Your Number's Up

Robert L Lambert

Your Number's Up

Robert Lambert

Paperback edition first published in the United Kingdom
in 2019 by aSys Publishing

eBook edition first published in the United Kingdom
in 2019 by aSys Publishing

Author photographed by Chris Lambert

Front cover design by author, painted by Paul Stanley

Disclaimer

This is a work of fiction. Names, characters, businesses, places,
events and incidents are either the products of the author's
imagination or used in a fictitious manner. Any resemblance to
actual persons, living or dead, or actual events
is purely coincidental.

ISBN: 978-1-07-093549-2

aSys Publishing
http://www.asys-publishing.co.uk

Dedicated to Ronéll

Chapter 1

He fired his gun, ripping through the faceless enemy, blood spattered in all directions. He could hear Jimbo in the back-ground shouting,

"Got your back Andy!"

There was an explosion. A blinding flash and a crack of thunder deafened them all. Debris was sent in all directions cutting down two members of his team. He heard their gasps of final breath and smelt burning flesh, as the shrapnel burned its way through to the bone. As the smoke cleared, he could see a pretty young woman and two children. The one child called for his Father and the young girl screamed 'Why'. The young woman eyes were full of despair with a single tear running down her cheek. She called his name as a car crashed through the wall, killing all three. Like a second bomb going off, body parts were sent in all directions, their beauty became a tangled mess of flesh, bone and blood. The driver got out laughing and pointed at Andrew,

1

"I've taken all you have, all you love … your family! and now I'm living in my hotel with all expenses paid for by you. It's time for you to wake up and smell the coffee Mr. A!" his laughter cut like a knife through his heart. The laughing cackle echoed in his mind as Andrew woke from the nightmare, which frequently visited him in various forms, when fueled by alcohol.

***

Andrew T. McIntosh had been sitting on his decking reading a newspaper article about the fatal hit and run which had happened on a Thursday whilst he had fallen asleep. He was a 'Thursday's Child', who had far to go! The irony did not allude him, neither did the bad dreams of the past!

Through the patio doors, his living room was cluttered, except for a chest of drawers, where the family photos of his young wife and two children took pride of place. There was one other photo of himself in his Military days. These were of his first family before he met the woman of his dreams. She was the one who kept his dreams sweet, now the dreams were nightmares. With him in the picture were two other colleagues taken after a successful desert covert operation in which hostages had been rescued. By that time, he had enjoyed a successful and colourful career, much of which went unsung, due to the secrecy of his teams operation. Despite this the Government official in charge of negotiations, was praised and later rewarded. The soldiers had to make do with a pay packet the size of the official's expences account.

That was many years ago. After leaving the forces he ran his own security firm made up of old military colleagues, bodyguards to the rich and famous. For five years this took him all over the world. In Germany, he met a beautiful girl who within seven months became his wife. A year later, their baby girl was born. Two years later a boy completed the family, so they moved to a bigger apartment overlooking the city. This was where Andy was now sitting, reading the newspaper article, as he had done over and over again. The article was dated 5th April 2014, exactly one year ago a mother and two young children who were shown in a photograph that matched the one on Andy's chest of drawers. They had been left for dead on a Thursday afternoon opposite a children's' playground. His son had survived with serious injuries but had been in a coma for the past 2 years. However, the previous day the Doctors had to inform him that the situation was hopeless. He took it well like any veteran, bottled it up deep inside, but it cut like a knife, disemboweling him and the pain burned.

There was a half empty bottle of scotch on the table next to Andy, a habit that had worsened over the past 2 years. He had not worked for those years, and like his colleagues, all of his savings were gone. They all had to move on and find paid work. The debt was mounting, there were the bills that he hadn't even opened. He once had it all! Now he was at a loss at losing it all. Not even the Army could have prepared him for what he felt now. In the field he had felt pain and fear, but this was hell in a modern world that should have been full of promise.

In his shirt pocket was a lottery ticket, which he had bought earlier that week from the same shop the scotch came from. Weekly Lottery was a habit he and his wife shared. Dreams of a seaside home, kids playing on the beach, and for him spending more time with the greatest love of his life . . . his family. In the background the TV news was full of corrupt politicians, rising crime statistics and society falling apart. Nothing in life made any sense anymore.

It was Saturday night which at one time would have been a fun night. Now all alone, it felt just like another night of drunken, self-pity, falling into a bottomless pit of despair. The empty glass he was holding fell out of his hand as he slipped into another listless sleep full of dreams which turned into nightmares.

***

The next morning after he drank much water and swallowed some headache pills for his hangover, whilst sipping at his mug of coffee he went on the internet to the Lotto site to check his numbers . . . 2,17,22,24,47,49 . . . It took a while for his mind to register . . . his thoughts seemed muddled as he realised that the numbers matched his lotto ticket! For a brief, second, he almost shouted out loud . . . then it dawned on him that he was alone.

He took a long-needed shower to try to clear his head and gather his thoughts . . . What to do next. The possibilities were endless. What would it take for him to feel better? He looked into the steamed-up mirror and asked himself out loud,

"You have won the lottery, so, why so glum? Get a grip man!"

But, it's hard to get inspired when the pain won't go away, the booze only ever coated it in a grey mist, giving him a fleeting moment of happiness, at the expense of his liver.

Later he did the necessary to claim his win of £6 Million and then he sat on his usual seat on the patio. He felt numb, with a vague sense of excitement.

***

On Monday, he wrote cheques and paid off his debts, occasionally he looked at the pictures of his family, who should have been there enjoying this with him. But he no immediate family, he was a lone child. Brought up by foster parents after a car accident killed his while he was 5 years old, at the time being looked after by a babysitter. His life had seemed like one big battle which had been made worse by foster parents who were very strict. Discipline was second nature when he joined the army at the age of 16. He wanted someone to blame for the loss of his family. Upon dissecting the situation, the driver of the car was protected by the lawyer. The judge had given a light sentence, but more so, the politicians who passed the laws. Those servants of the many, who abused the very people who paid their salaries. He then realised that the only thing that would make his life whole was revenge, by being that bitter, the fruit seemed much sweeter ... Revenge for the death of his family.

He dug out another newspaper article that covered the capture of the person responsible for his pain ... ... Guilty as charged!

What good did that do when the accused had served only 18 months? "Good behavior" and a "maverick" young lawyer, was all it had taken.

He poured a scotch and downed it in one. He looked at the bottle then at the picture of his wife, putting the top back on the bottle he vowed not to have another drop until his first mission was complete. That night he had more nightmares, he dreamt of all his old comrades who were standing alongside his family, they were all chanting, 'move-on, move-on, the past is the past.'

Chapter 2

The next three weeks were spent on a military style fitness regime with the diet that his body had missed. The alcohol withdrawal symptoms were strong at times; however, his determination was even stronger.

Whenever he lost focus, he would start cleaning the apartment and within a week it was spotless which added to his sense of achievement. Day by day he became more focused, until he found David Conway, the drunk driver who wiped out his family.

***

Conway was not working, he was claiming benefits and was living in a small flat in the middle of town. Andy stalked him . . . day in and day out. Patience was his friend, and time his ally. Giving him space to think and plan, . . . until the time was right.

It was raining when David Conway left his council flat, he carried an old umbrella with a cane handle, he walked at a fast pace, as the rain got heavier. Andy followed him, he felt at home in the warm rain, it reminded him of tropical weather and all-night maneuvers.

Conway stopped, and entered a bargain booze shop where he bought a strong cider and cigarettes, then headed back to his flat. Andy followed, closing the space between them. He knew that an alleyway was coming up ahead. As soon as Conway was at the alleyway entrance, Andy pounced pulling him into it. Within seconds several punches, and a head lock followed by a quick upward jerk, Conway was coughing blood . . . it was all over. Andy took the cigarettes, the cider and his money, making the scene look like a robbery. He quickly made his way back to his car along the empty streets.

He saw a crippled homeless man in a doorway and stopped. He gave him the cider, cigarettes . . . and the money.

"Here, take these. I know what it feels like to be down on one's luck."

The tramp thought it was Christmas, he looked up and smiled. Andy hurried home . . . And once inside, he promptly vomited in the sink. He had killed the enemy many times as a soldier, but this was very different. Now he had been Judge, Jury and Executioner to a civilian, not an enemy soldier. He had given so many of his years as a soldier, to supporting and upholding the system. A system that was not now supporting him. He looked at the framed pictures of his family and quietly pleaded with them.

"Please forgive me, I had to do this, the world has gone mad since you've been gone. I want a life again! Besides real justice had to be given out! The system has gone soft."

He opened a cupboard and pulled out a half empty bottle of scotch and poured a glass then downed it. It felt good, biting and warm inside, he had not touched booze in a while.

It took away the sting of what he had just done. There he was, with a whole pile of cash in the bank and no debts. He should be the happiest guy alive, yet he felt sick to the stomach. He poured one drink after the other and sat in the armchair, hoping it would take the pain and sickness away. He looked at the pictures on the wall of him in his military days. Then his eyes were drawn to the newspaper, the political scandals that seemed to dominate the news. The people that would send him and his colleagues on dangerous missions, in the name of "Queen and Country" sat back with their cocktails and their feet up on their fat wallets. He remembered his best friend disappearing as an explosion blew him into a thousand pieces, only one boot had remained where he been standing, smoldering with the heat and smelling of death. That smell was something you never forget or ever got accustomed to. He still had many contacts, and now with the cash he could start his own one-man war; maybe even change the country, put a different headline on those daily papers. Where Guy Faulks failed, he could pick up the pieces. Except his would be a military operation with many objectives. It would not just be a load of politicians he would blow up. He would select those individuals who were not only tarnished with a little scandal, but those big king rats that were rotten to the core.

In the past, he had been involved with bringing down dictators, this was no different, and the reward would not be money.

He poured another drink, but this time with a smile, because now he felt he had a purpose . . . he would use his new wealth to put right what he saw as wrong. His first task was to attain the tools for the job, much of his gear he could get via the internet, but guns he would have to source from somewhere that could not be traced . . . the criminal underworld. His eyes grew tired as he got out of his chair, he picked up the empty bottle of scotch and put it in the recycling bin, then made himself a coffee. He switched on his computer and sipped the coffee. He spent the next two hours online buying numerous items, then he set off to the local shops to buy more items and a daily paper. Andy paid for his goods and left browsing a newspaper. One of the stories was of a politician who was often in the paper for wasting public money and abusing his position. This story linked him to being sympathetic to a foreign power which supported terrorism. He looked like the type of man who would sell his own Grandmother. Derek James was in the papers nearly every week for one thing or another and had been moved from one position to another, yet he still managed to hold a position of power. Andy smiled, for this was to be his second target. This would have to be subtle. He did not want to put them all on alert, he did not want any panic in the ranks after just one victim. His eyes fell on a short article at the bottom of the page, a body was found in an alley in the center of town, robbery looked to be a possible motive. Next of kin were yet to be found and informed, the Police were appealing for witnesses.

***

When he arrived home, he started his research to find out everything he could about Derek James. He then packed a bag for a day's outing, he was to pose as a freelance journalist to gain other information he needed. Andy was methodical about planning, as a plan well thought out, was a successful mission.

He drove for an hour, and then stopped at a local shop asking for Derek James whereabouts.

"He lives in the next village." replied the shopkeeper, "Big place called The Oaks, he's got security gates mind! He hates you lot! Reporters!"

"Does he use your shop?"

"As if? He wouldn't be caught dead in here."

"Well you never know." Andy replied trying not to laugh at the shop keeper's choice of words.

"Never!" said the shop keeper, "He's not local, he's from the city. Plans for an extension on his house got passed, though the previous owners were refused. It's who you know, in this world, the rest of us can go and jump."

"Well that could be true. So, he does not like Reporters?"

"Politicians often don't. He does get a lot of foreign visitors I hear. His gardener uses this shop. Nice old boy, who was a soldier in his youth. Mind you, at his age he shouldn't be working, and I bet that wanker only pays him a pittance."

"You mean below the minimum wage." replied Andy.

"I think so, but the old guy needs the money and half-a-loaf is better than none ... That's his way of thinking."

"Do you know his name and where he lives?"

Andy wrote down the details, then left the shop in search of the old soldier called Ted Benson.

***

The door was answered by the little man. Andy explained that he was doing research on the area, and was invited in. Inside it was a small bed-sit, kept beautifully clean. The bed was freshly made with hospital corners. A picture of the Queen was on the wall next to some service medals. Andy asked him,

"May I call you Ted? I would love to get into the grounds of The Oaks. It has a great deal of local history to it, but Mr. James is not interested in allowing us access ... very private for such a public man. I was hoping you could help. It will be worth £1000 cash for you!"

The little man looked stunned at the offer.

"You must make a lot of money from this writing to afford that?"

"Ok! You drive a hard bargain Ted, £2000." he said with a wink. Ted smiled.

Andy took a liking him immediately, as he reminded him of his own Father.

Ted had just had one question. "What day?"

"Tomorrow? If you give me his phone number, I will phone him tonight and arrange my visit."

***

At 6.30pm Andy telephoned Derek James,

"Mr. Derek James, my name is Dawson, Charles Dawson from the BBC. I am making a special documentary about celebrities and their gardens and I would like to open the program with your period garden, which I am informed has many exquisite trees and landscaping that beautifully depicts a Manor Garden. I would welcome the opportunity to visit tomorrow and discuss this with you and your grounds man. Make notes for various camera angles and of course if possible, an interview with yourself."

"Interview me! Well I'm sure my man can help you and I will be around, so we can arrange a convenient date for my performance." He chuckled, thinking of his face gracing the Radio Times.

The following day Andy returned to Ted's. Inside his jacket was a small

digital camera and recorder to make notes. He told Ted of the telephone conversation and the cover story which Ted agreed that it was a good cover. Walking into the grounds of the house Andy made discreet note of the security system, cameras, ground layout and the garage, which seemed to have no fancy locks, and there was even a convenient window at the side. They were relying on the gate with code entry only. The house was a different story, it seemed tighter than a drum, but this did not bother Andy, as his plans did not involve the house, or any of Derek James family. Ted showed Andy around the grounds pointing out the various trees and shrubs, and also gave him a brief history. During this time, Andy was planning his next course of action. They had just finished the tour when they noticed Derek James leaving the house. He was just about to open his garage door when he noticed them and started to make his way over. When about ten feet away he called out,

"Morning Ted, who is this?"

"He's from the BBC, he said that he's spoken to you."

Andy could pick up vibes from Ted that he was intimidated by his boss. So, he put on his best voice and offered a handshake, "I'm Charles, we spoke last night regarding the celebrity special."

Those few words sent a tingle down Derek James back, feeding his ego to bursting point.

"My dear fellow, pleasure to meet you. I'm sure my man will show you everything you need to see, for your camera angles. There's a rather lovely bush over there that's in full bloom, where you can film me. I can get my wife to lay on sandwiches and tea for the film crew" he chirped, acting like a Hollywood icon.

"Ted here, is my gardener."

Then he raised his voice at Ted, to imply he was a little deaf.

"You do alright, don't you Ted . . . but at times a little slow."

He then turned back on Ted, winked at Andy with a smirk grin,

"He's handy to have around, like a small smelly dog to get rid of the vermin. I pay him enough to live off, after all he gets his pension, works for both of us! I mean what else would he do at that age! It's up to us gentry to employ the less fortunate of the village. Do our bit, so to speak, I'm sure you'll agree! Any way I must be off! I will leave you with Ted now as I'm needed in Parliament. You can speak to my secretary about setting a date, here's my card. I also have a previous appointment with my building developer."

Andy cringed as Derek James walked away. Ted looked up at Andy, his small frame once athletic, now quite frail,

"He means well, but he just can't help being a right pompous twit at times. His building developer friend is a right sort! Much worse in fact!"

They carried on walking the grounds, although Andy had seen enough, he listened to Teds anecdotes of his life story. Something he guessed he didn't get to divulge too often with people, he could see he was enjoying it, so Andy let him offload his story.

***

Later in Ted's bed sit, Andy handed him a thick brown envelope which he opened. It had £5000 inside it. Andy with a wink explained that he could never count, which brought a warm smile to Ted's face who with both hands shook Andy's. Then Andy asked,

"What did you mean about his development friend was a right sort?"

"He's well known for buying lovely properties from desperate people and those who, shall we say, a little slow and old. Taking advantage of them. Then knocking the places down and replacing them with cheap homes, built with cheap labour, as well as skirting health & safety requirements. Men have even been badly injured on his sites I hear!! My nephew has worked on his sites in the past and has told me of bribes exchanging hands and even bribery using call girls to set-up unsuspecting property owners. He's managed to buy farms and turn them into housing estates with his Lordships blessing and support. He's as crooked as my spine."

"Your spine?"

"Yes, damn arthritis and old age they call it. But my mind is still sharp as a tack, I just don't let him know that. I know he uses me and thinks I'm some sort of slave, but the cash is jolly useful, and I get this little place rent free. It was once a small gate house. I know it's no bigger than a person's office, but from the outside it looks quite posh!"

Andy looked around at his home that was no better than a tiny bedsit.

"What's this developers name?"

"James Richardson."

He then named a few of the farms that had disappeared, one of which Andy remembered as a young lad, where he and his girl, who later became his wife would go walking.

"James Richardson, taker of homes and farms, odd to think it was not that long ago the Government said that they would never build on farmland. This island of ours is getting smaller, before we know it the countryside will be gone. Then what? What will be left for the young generations? Nothing but bloody computer games, and drugs to escape a shrinking world."

Andy was taken aback by this little old man's shrewd out-look on the world around him.

"You could be right Ted!"

"Is this what I fought a war for. End up in a bedsit, ruled over by an arrogant snob, and sneered at by lazy adolescent youngsters."

"No Ted, it's not. But things may change?"

"I hope you are right."

Andy had seen and heard enough of Derek James for one day and left for home. On the way, back he stopped off at a motorcycle shop and chose an almost new Honda 600cc bike, complete with helmet and leather jacket. Buying it all by debit card, he put the receipt with owner certificate in the inside pocket of the new jacket. He rode it back whilst his car was parked in the shop's car park with the agreement to pick it up within a week. When he got home, he downloaded the pictures he had taken and took notes from the few recorders notes he had made. He poured a scotch, laid out the printed pictures and his notes. He decided that his hits would carry an obvious message and should also carry a symbol, so he turned to a A4 sketch pad and with a thick felt pen. He started doodling ideas, then drew out a letter A for Andy, putting it inverted and removing the middle bar it became a V. On his computer was a graphics program, so he produced and printed out a letter A that filled the page. He then cut out the bar, leaving a distinctive pattern that easily showed where it came from and stuck it on the bottom, so now the A also read as a V. A cryptic message stating A is for Victory. He saw it as a game, a puzzle to give the police, but more importantly to prove he had killed the subject. He started to print it off by placing his image in a scanner and printing out many photocopies. He sipped the scotch then lay back in his armchair to contemplate his next plan of action. His plan was to screw one up an A4 sheet and leave it in the mouth of the body, he thought it would speak volumes!

The James house was secure, the family were not to be hurt, so the only way to avoid them being near was to strike when he wasn't home, but in his car. He knew of many ways to make it look like an accident, however did he want to? He had planned originally not to send a message nor create any pattern ... but now he was thinking, why waste a good death.

Chapter 3

The following morning, when he woke everything had been laid out by him in his bedroom the night before in a regimental fashion. Andy had a light breakfast with coffee. Dressed in jeans, a leather jacket he picked up a small ruck sack that he had previously packed.

Riding off to Derek James's house he parked just up the road from the ornate main gate. Andy waited until he was leaving in his silver Mercedes car. He followed at a safe distance until a long stretch of road came up and then overtook at speed along the country road and raced to the brow of a hill. He had noted at this point that in the road there was a sharp right-hand bend. He parked in a farm field entrance and from his backpack he quickly laid down 8 strips of thick plywood each 18 inches long, 8 inches wide with 4-inch nails pointing up. The silver Mercedes came past soon after over the hill and hit the nails. Two front tyres blew, wood flew into the wheel arches and the disc brake system, making the car swerve out of control. The steering wheel spun from side to side with

James franticly trying to correct the car. But the speed made it impossible, missing the bend in the road and shot violently into a hedge. The air bag went off in his face which made him gasp for air and his heart race. James was dazed, but alive, until Andy opened the driver's door,

"Time to pay the ferryman, your days of stamping on the weak are over!"

Then he calmly smothered his face, James tried to struggle, and grabed at Andy's jacket, but the clawing became weak until he eventually stopped breathing. Andy calmly screwed up the A4 cryptic letter and pushed it into James mouth. He got back on his bike he rode off before any another vehicle turned up.

Mixed emotions ran through his mind, this time he felt a wave of exhilaration running through his veins. He hit the main road once more heading for home, and came across a young man with a broken-down motorbike, sitting on the verge with his helmet removed. For a moment the young man reminded him of what his son could have grown into, which made his parental feelings kick in. He pulled up and asked if he needed help.

"Are you ok?"

"Not really, my bike has just died on me. I was warned it may happen last time when it was in the bike shop. I think it's bad, it was making a hell of a knocking noise."

"Sounds like your big ends gone, very expensive."

The young man burst into tears and Andy sat down next to him,

"Nothing's that bad, is it?"

"Oh yes, it is ... it really is!"

Andy was taken aback that someone so young and clean cut was so desperate.

"There's a café just round the next bend or two . . . we could go and get a coffee? Bring your helmet, hop on and we'll take it from there."

"Really! Cheers, I really need one!"

Once they arrived at the café and were sitting drinking their coffee's, the young man became more composed,

"I was on my way home to Glasgow to see my Mum. She's been ill, and I've been working in London as a dispatch rider, that's why the bikes knackered. The pay is crap, so I could not keep a roof over my head or keep the bike going, so I decided to go back home and nurse my Mum, but now I can't even do that. I tried to save money working locally for a building developer James Richardson Limited, but the pay was worse than average and was conned into overtime which I never got paid for. Seems the turnover of staff was great, mostly EU workers."

Andy saw the distress in his eyes,

"I've heard of this company before, none of it's good."

"His foremen was no better than a thug, with limited building skills, who shouldn't even be left alone with Lego!"

Andy's head was spinning, he felt a need to make something right, this night. They got back on the bike and rode back to his car and the young man got off, and as Andy got off, he handed him the keys.

"Take my bike and this jacket it's your size . . . just! Helmet too, yours looks a little worn to say the least."

The young man looked in total shock,

"But I can't afford this!" almost shaking.

But then Andy made him make a promise.

"I'm letting you take this under one condition. Live with your Mum and take diligent care of her until you have something better sorted out. Maybe dispatch riding up there. This bike will serve you well, and take this, it's only a few hundred quid but it's enough for fuel. This is my gift to you, so you don't owe me anything, just honour my wishes and make a life for yourself."

"Are you rich?"

"I was once, this is only money. Wealth takes on many shapes and forms, not all true rich's have pound signs. You'll find that out one day."

The young man did not know what to say,

"But why? You don't know me."

"You don't need to know someone to see when they need help."

They signed all the paperwork and Andy handed him the keys.

"Ride safe!"

Andy then got into his car and drove home with a sense of achievement. He saw that he had taken one life and had saved another.

***

On the way back, he stopped in a layby and used his mobile to Google James Richardson Limited. He also found a link on the following page to a blog, clearly stating that Richardson Limited should be avoided. But others contested such views! Andy felt this could easily be put on behalf of Richardson's, but there is never smoke without fire.

It didn't take long, and his office was on the way home, so he called in to pose as a possible customer wanting a house built. At the company's office he was surprised to find a pretty young receptionist who looked if she had been crying,

"Sorry to interrupt, have I called in at a wrong moment, I was hoping to get some advice on a building project I have planned."

"I'm sorry Mr. Richardson has left for the day and I must go too, it's my last day ... it seems!"

"It seems ... Why?"

"I've just been sacked."

"I'm sorry."

"If I was you, I wouldn't use this company, he's a cowboy and a bloody pervert."

"Well that spoke volumes. Thank you my dear and may I wish you well in your job hunting."

"Now I must lock up and put the keys through the letter box, so I have to ask you to leave. I'm sorry I can't be of more help."

"No need to apologise, you've been more helpful than you realise." she had highlighted the reasons why Richardson deserved to be on the list.

He also wished he could do something for her, she had unknowingly helped to make his mind up about Mr. Richardson's fate.

He decided to return the next day, early. He parked next to a nearly new Bentley which had private number plates that was obviously Richardson's.

He entered to find the reception empty, but Richardson could be seen through his open office door, he knocked on the door,

"Good morning! There was no receptionist, but I saw your that door was opened, so knocked."

"That's OK, I gave the receptionist the day off to see her sick Mother." Andy knew that to be a lie. Richardson carried on with more lies,

"I like to look after all my employees, it's so important, don't you agree."

"Indeed, pay them well and get good results. Happy staff makes happy customers through good service and products." replied Andy

"Exactly! Now then, how can I help?"

"I'm looking for a builder to renovate a property I have outside Oxford. I have just inherited from a wealthy Aunt. It stands on a small holding of about six acres. Just on the outskirts of a little Cotswold village of Broadway. Do you know it?"

He sat in a chair in front of Richardson's desk and put his briefcase down in front of it. He could sense the excitement flowing from him, as he knew the area oozed wealth. Money with a capital M!

"You've come to the right place then sir. I have a great team of experts all highly qualified in such projects. Do you have plans with you or ideas of your needs?" rubbing his hands together at the thought of six acres of possible building land in a prime location for London commuters, with lots of money. "6 acres you say, that takes a great deal of hard work and upkeep. Had you considered selling and putting the money into a new property, I might be able to help you with the sale and purchase. No estate agent's fees saving you money! Of course, land prices are down now, but we could come to an arrangement?"

"Interesting thought, maybe have the work done on the house and sell you the land to help pay for the work. I will go away and think about this, thanks for your ideas. I will return tomorrow with the plans. Let's say about 4pm"

"I'll look forward to seeing them, because of course with all the pit falls these days where modification and restoration is involved. It's a nightmare, but with our experience, we can take care of all that for you for a nominal fee of course. The various taxes, architects' fees, materials, labour will all have to be considered obviously, but we do all that for you. Re-modelling old building into exquisite homes is our business. But of course, it depends on which route you want to go down, either restoration or sell to me and buy new, which I could supply for you locally, nearer your business."

"Food for thought, see you tomorrow!"

Andy stood up and reached across and shook his hand and then he left the office. Richardson was so engrossed about the prospect that he didn't notice Andy had left the briefcase, which was in front of his desk. As he drove off, he checked his rear-view mirror, then triggered the contents of the briefcase. The explosion ripped through the building as Richardson was about to drink a toast to himself.

"I do believe your office needs re-modeling now Mr. Richardson!

***

Meanwhile Mr. James's car was the subject of scrutiny by the police. They had cordoned off the road, while the Pathologist and the forensic team worked. It was clearly not an accident. The pathologist informed the detective that Mr. James had suffocated. When asked if the air bag was to blame, he replied,

"No! They're designed to save lives, not take them. There were deaths years ago of small children which was due to their size and that's why they are not allowed in the front anymore. Mr. James being an adult was in reasonable heath by the looks of him, not overweight and middle aged he should have survived. I will know more after an autopsy; I would guess who ever laid those nailed planks came to this open-door window and finished him off. Quite a cold killer."

"You should be a detective Doc!"

"No thanks, the dead give me the information and I relay it to you. It's your job to find out why someone went to great lengths to kill him. Why not make him pull over and steal an expensive car? Why after killing him not take his wallet?"

The young detective looked bemused as his senior came along side after hearing the discussion,

"Take note of the docs suggestions sergeant, as he makes good valid points. Hi, Doc, how's business these days!"

"Dead! Yours?"

"Never a quiet moment, business is on the up. So, you reckon our Mr. James was murdered."

"That's for you to decide when you get my full report."

At this point the doc found the piece of paper in Mr. James mouth and opened it before slipping it into an evidence bag,

"Detectives, the plot thickens with a note that has a V or A on it!"

Chapter 4

***

The following day he researched a man he was already familiar with from past scandals, a man who had (in Andy's eyes) been rewarded with a knighthood for making fifteen thousand people redundant. Mr. Brown was asked to cut costs within a very large company, so he shut down all high street offices at the cost of 20,000 jobs and set up internet direct only business, which did not give the best value for money in comparison to the high street system, it was open to corruption. He was also known for being a bully to his staff, and repugnant to female staff, who had to accept his sexual remarks and groping ways, or be shown the door. In one newspaper article pictures were taken of the new female dress code on which he had insisted, he said it showed corporate image. A sexy image of smoky haze tights under a short red skirt with red stiletto heels. Topped with a cropped pinstripe red jacket emphasizing their waist and a black silky blouse. The photographs resembled a magazine "top shelf style", which certainly caught the eyes of some men, but scorned by feminist action groups. Sir Peter Brown, as he liked to be called, loved to see his female staff when he visited each office and shop, around the country. His favorite hobby was to check each of the female staff out, then make a list of the ones that took his eye. Each Christmas these staff members were invited to a party under the impression that their name had been chosen at random. They were to attend with all expenses paid, including overnight stay. Brown was well known to bed at least one of these women during those parties, with the others were seen as fair game for his high-powered friends, of whom, not all worked for the company.

Andy had read a large article on Brown written by a reporter who stated that these parties were now every month and not just at Christmas. Given the fancy title of Team Building Reviews. The young girls were not aware of what TBR's meant and went like lambs to the slaughter. One such girl was Jane MacDonald, a pretty 17-year-old. Eager to do well in life and make her parents proud, especially her Dad Tom, a policeman who doted on her. At one such party she was abused by Brown himself after a date rape drug was slipped in her drink. He had been careful and only a tiny amount so she was aware of everything that happened. But was powerless to fight him off, it all seemed like a dream. Janes was robbed of her innocence, what should have been a beautiful experience with someone she loved became a nightmare.

Her father found out after she became silent and withdrawn. Official reports were made, but no evidence was found as she had stood in a shower for over an hour trying to wash away the filth, but no matter how much she had scrubbed she could still feel his presence. It was of little relief that he had used a condom, it meant there was no evidence she had been raped. The mental scar grew inside her over the proceeding 18months that ate away at her soul was very evident. She became withdrawn and tearful, until her Farther, Tom, received news that her body had been found hanging in a wood. The case never even got to court, because of the lack of forensic evidence, but Janes final words to her father as she retired to bed, the night before she took her own life were burned into Toms memory,

"Daddy I'm sorry, but Brown ruined my life, and it will not wash away."

***

Sir Peter Brown was indeed the next target and Andy had a plan. The infamous parties were held at the same place every time. On such a night Andy stole a waiter's outfit and used it to posed as an agency waiter. He worked alongside the rest of the staff, who were completely oblivious of Andy's lack of knowledge and of making cocktails. Beers and shorts were fine, but cocktails were a mystery to him. After a few hours of free drinks being consumed and the buffet table being emptied, various items of clothing were starting to be loosened. Black bowties clung around the necks of silver tongued men, who's dialogue had become more colourful with their increasing bravado. Hands disappeared up the women's skirts, some were received with encouragement, and others with a slap. Towards the end of the evening Brown and "friends" were all quite the worst for wear. Andy crept into the room where a young girl lay unconscious, Brown was on top of her using her from behind. Her stockings were torn, and her clothing was scattered over the room. Andy came up behind the couple and produced a knife, which he had hidden against his ankle. He held it to Brown's throat,

"Get up Fatso." He ordered Brown, and marched him to the bathroom and made him kneel in front of the toilet. From the back of his trousers, Andy produced a cable tie, where he slipped it over both of Brown's wrists which were behind his back. Then with his knee on his back and using gaffer tape, Andy stuck Browns head across the toilet. Meantime, Brown pleaded and offered him money to let him go. The figure reached £50k for his freedom, but Andy replied. Even £50K was rejected

"What value do you put on a young girl's life?"

"What young girl?" Uttered Brown

"You see, you can't even remember. The pain you are about to feel will be nothing compared to all the pain you have inflicted on so many innocent people."

Andy without emotion Andy cut one side of Brown's throat. The blood started spurted out and ran into the toilet pan at a steady pace.

"You will watch as your life goes down the toilet. If you scream and panic, the faster the flow of blood, the quicker you will die. Now, will you take the chance that you'll be found or will you scream for help, which might fall on deaf ears, as most of you friends are so pissed, and the girls are all knocked out by your spiked drinks and the waiter staff are now gone for the night...you may have about five minutes to make your peace with God, although I don't rate your luck at the Pearly gates!"

"You bastard!" Growled Brown and as Andy got up and he left to the sounds of Brown's desperate pleas of,

"Oh God, Oh God." and in a drunken state his friend across the landing faintly heard him and replied,

"Go for it Peter, give her a what for!" then collapsed onto his bed next to a ravaged young girl. Browns brief cries for help, turned into a gurgle, within five minutes all went silent, but those five minutes were the longest for Sir Peter Brown.

Andy went back into the bedroom and took a knife that had been used for cutting the young girl's clothes off. He used it to pin the A4 paper with the letter A to his Brown's back. The handle of the knife had a Masons symbol on it, which made Andy smile with the irony as he slowly pushed it into his victims back,

"You used it on her, now the symbol that you worship has stabbed you in the back to send, sending a message to all the others. Give my regards to Satan."

That night Andy slept uneasily, experiencing a mixture of nightmares from his lost family, to fallen comrades in arms, he had lucid dream of is wife who asked him what he was doing. In the morning he woke and went to the local shop, when returned he sat in his chair with the daily paper and a cup of coffee. The first few pages told a story of a Hollywood scandal, a large house fire that killed an entire family, followed by the latest gossip on the Royal family. Page four was different, it told of a Politician linked to child porn, an accusation of which he strongly denied. The story also went on to say that he had been accused of receiving gifts and bribes for his support of dodgy building developments, of which he also denied, even though the reporter had dug up a witness to support the allegation. That same witness was later found dead after falling from a tall building. In his pocket a typed suicide note. Andy decided to investigate the politician whose name was Colin Barnard, and his previous whereabouts and movements. He sat at the computer and finished his coffee. All the info appeared on the screen including a postal address.

He found more stories about the politician, old ones of accusations and rumours of corruption, as well as a messy divorce where his wife accused him of using rent boys. No court case was ever made, he had many friends in high places, quite possibly many of whom were also corrupt. Colin Barnard was going to be next, but this time he would make sure the message was sent and received.

Browns body was discovered by cleaning staff that morning alongside a hysterical half clothed young lady. The pathologist recognized the letter which had been attached to Browns back. Immediately in a quiet tone, he spoke to the detective and his sergeant,

"It's the same note by the look of it, but the manner in which he was killed, is very disturbing. It would have taken Mr. Brown at least 5 minutes to die. The killer purposely cut only one side of his neck in such a way, so to the lengthen the time it took for the victim to die."

"If he's leaving notes, then we can expect more, this killer is on a mission."

***

Later, whilst Andy was on the road driving to the address he found on the net, the place turned out to be Barnards office. Posing as a reporter who was researching an article on local government, he found that this ploy had worked successfully last time and seemed a perfect way to ask probing questions. Inside the premises were two people who helped with his running of daily admin who seemed more than willing to divulge information on their boss. Both were young girls who were smartly dressed who resembled fashion catwalk models, both seemed to have a naive outlook on life. The pretty blonde girl told him that Barnard was a bit of a letch who could not resist brushing up against her at every opportunity. The other girl, a brunette complained that he often asked them to come on trips to various places, with the dubious task of doing administration work. Each time they had both managed to find excuses, but his patience was wearing thin. He became more bad tempered after their constant refusals. Each girl was making plans to move on to a new life away from his advances. They also told Andy that they believed many of the rumours of Barnard to be true. Some of his visitors were very strange, to say the least. The blonde was convinced he was a drug dealer, as he was quite well known around the local night club scene.

Andy felt as if he had struck gold. The information was so forthcoming and compelling, they even gave their employers up to date home address and car registration. They saw it as retribution for all the harassment he had put them through and the hardship and exceptionally low pay they were given.

They then requested,

"Please do not let it slip where all this information came from, we need these jobs until at least we have new ones to go to."

Andy assured them that their identities would be safe with him, which of course it would be.

"After all ladies I don't know your names. I wish you both good luck with finding other work."

He left the office with his small recorder was full of details. He headed off to Barnards home address, which was situated in an exclusive apartment block, fronted by large electronic gates, security cameras and a coded front door lock which required a pass key. He sighed,

"I thought it was going a little too well, this calls for a long stake out in the car."

31

He parked the car in a place which gave a clear view of the apartment block. He then walked to a nearby shop to buy a magazine, sandwiches and a drink. He sat back in his car multitasking. He ate and drank whilst he browsed the magazine and also keeping an eye on the people going in and coming out of the premises. It was approaching 6.30pm when Barnard appeared. He was alone and carrying a briefcase after he had parked his Porsche. He took a card from his inside pocket, he swiped the door lock making it bleep and then entered. Andy checked the car registration then waited until he saw a light come on to signifying the location of Barnards apartment. He saw enough, and made his way home, his mind methodically mulled over all the details and possibilities. He knew that he had to source a firearm, and a good one. He had his sights on a Precision Guided firearm or a PGF for short, a XS1, at 27 inches long weighing 20lb loaded with a home in targeting system which only fired when it knew it would hit its target. An intelligent snipers' rifle that he could obtain from the USA. But how? He had one contact, an old service friend that legally dealt in firearms, he may, if the price was right, might be able to get the gun for him. It meant his friend, Jimbo, would need to keep it secret, however, he did feel that Jimbo would.

***

That night he lay in bed, planning his next endeavour. He looked at the bedside clock, it was 11.00pm. He reached for his mobile and called Jimbo.

"Hi Jimbo. Its Andy. Yes, fine mate and yes long time since we spoke. Jimbo I have a favour to ask you. Is it possible to get a certain rifle for me from the States that's not exactly Kosher? The XS1 in fact."

Jimbo went quiet, Andy could hear his mind ticking over, then Jimbo replied, "Possible...but it will cost, well over twenty grand and getting into the country via the back door could cost more! You're talking a lot of money Andy. You shitting money these days?" he laughed

"No, I have come into some money."

"Nice one! So why the gun Andy, are you aiming on pissing someone off?"

"No...Going hunting."

"Well you can't miss with that baby. Fuck it tells your iPad when you've made the hit. Really cool shit! Let me see what I can come up with. I mean, there are plenty of good sniper rifles out there that cost a fraction of that beast, and easier to get."

"I'll leave it your capable hands. See you tomorrow."

***

Next morning Andy pulled up at Jimbo's and was greeted with a man hug, considering that Jimbo was over two meters tall and the size of a house was a bit unsettling, even for Andy. In the service, it used to be the standing joke that when parachuting, that Jimbo needed his own plane and specially made parachute. Yet the whole team were always at ease on a mission they knew that they had the Black Hulk on their side. His parents, Irish Mother and Jamaican Father, had died when he was young. The service became his entire world, the regiment were his family and his team his brothers, with Jeremy being his sister. He was openly gay when not in uniform, but no one cared, they were family, and watched each other's back. At parties Jeremy was the life and soul, and a great cook, but when in uniform he was as lethal as the next man.

Jimbo made coffee and showed him a picture that took pride of place next to a display of the very finest of gentlemen's shotguns.

"Remember this pic, you and me and the guy's in Iraq. Fun and games eh! We could have done with a few XS1's then"

"Good times Jimbo."

They were joined by Jimbo's German Sheppard dog, Duke who, immediately recognising Andy as a friend, jumped up on the seat and rested his head on Andy's lap, letting him stroke his head.

"This gun you want. Yes, I can get it. Give me three weeks. Now I'm not going to preach to you, hell I know you man, just be careful."

The next hour was full of anecdotes of their service days, then it was time for Andy to leave,

"I will wait to hear from you."

"Roger that Andy." Jimbo replied looking at the photo once more, then he added, "Andy, whatever it is. If you ever need help, just pick up the phone. I'm bored with civvy life, pansy rich buggers coming in here with shit loads of cash, or gold cards paying out for shotguns, so they can shoot some poor sodding defenseless duck. If a mercenary is on the right side and the money is good, I'm game. I mean, I gave the best years of my life to this country, but the sodding government ... Well you know, promises made and broken."

"Yes, I know, we thought our Generals were in charge, but the Politician's from behind their cozy desks always won. Sending us into situations with crap gear, and leant back in a nice leather chairs, smoking endless cigars thinking they've solved all the world's problems ... Pricks! Their average pay is over £60,000 a year or more, plus huge expenses allowances and no doubt backhanders in some cases, nearly three times that of the guy fighting on the front line. Life to them is cheap, we lost many for bad causes that made no sense, a soldier needs to believe in what he does."

***

Andy drove away giving Jimbo the thumbs up, and Jimbo returned the gesture unsure whether if his close friend was on the verge of a breakdown. He had never known him to be this way before.

On the way home Andy thought of Jimbo's last request, he was a little tempted to tell his close friend, yet it could get him killed, or life in prison. It was his hate of injustice that fueled his anger.

He arrived home after coming to terms that Barnard's assassination would have to go on hold until the arrival of the XS1 rifle, or at least the best Jimbo could get. He had already planned that the advantage point from a hill, half a klick from Barnards house would give a perfect sight for a sniper's rifle. He would have left the house and out of sight of children's eyes.

So, for now he decided to make the most of his available time, and relocate to a country house. He found one set on the outskirts of a small village which possessed one small shop & post office with the local pub next door. It had security powered iron gates and a 100-yard pebble drive that swept round to the front door hidden away from the lane. The garden that surrounded the property was over an acre, with a brick and stone wall that marked its perimeter. He noticed when perusing the grounds that there was an old oak door in the one wall at the bottom of the garden, hidden by ivy overgrowth. He saw it as a useful escape route especially with natural camouflage. Inside the house, it was tidy and needed no work at all, much to Andy's pleasure. A large double garage and a work-shop stood to one side, and was surrounded by mature trees and shrubs, giving privacy from the road. Upstairs in one of the two large double bedrooms he imagined his family enjoy-ing life there, if only he could turn the clock back, the sound of the kids running in and out of the three bedrooms. His wife walking out of the bathroom with a towel rapped round her head, pulling it off and bending forwards, shaking her long dark hair and then flicking it back with a smile that melted his heart every time.

"Miss you honey." He muttered. "Miss you all."

***

Meanwhile in the local morgue the detective could not see a connection between the victims, this left everyone perplexed. However, the Pathologist in a serious tone remarked to his assistant,

"I have a horrible feeling we will see more of these in the near future."

"Serial killer?"

"To qualify as a serial killer requires three killings. This killer is accurate, cold and calculating, with some sort of agenda. Yes, we could be looking at a potential serial killer, but for once I would like to be wrong."

Back at Andy's new home he was putting his skills and money to good use. He had CCTV security system fitted, a fully kitted workshop in the garage next to his new car, a black Land Rover Sports he found on eBay. He picked it up from Birmingham, and fitted it with extra spot lamps, satellite navigation, and a dashboard cam which could relay pictures to an on-board pc fitted in the back. He hid tightly bound plastic bags, money in £10,000 bundles, just in-case his access to cash became a problem. Because Bank accounts were being frozen by authorities, it was not a future impossibility. He also stocked up a storeroom with all sorts of equipment and supplies that he may need on any of his assignments, the title he now gave to any target, each day he would go through the papers and started several files on politicians. But his eyes started to be drawn to heads of industry who seemed to show a complacent attitude to the cutbacks in the work force, whilst giving themselves large pay rises. When asked by one reporter on the subject, a Mr. Jonathon Bale replied,

"It's not as much as you think, it's because of my contract."

This was true; however, he had a hand in the re-writing of his own contract, making him a cool £1.5 million each year. His story was not original, the more Andy looked the more he found. There were people in what were government funded companies, who earned a lot more than the Prime Minister, for working less hours.

He decided to walk to the pub a mile down the road. He soon found himself making friends with the locals but kept his past and his wealth a secret. He decided that taking early retirement after selling his internet company sounded good, and plausible story for his identity in the pub. The pub interior was unchanged since the 70's, red flock wallpaper, nicotine stained magnolia paint, and a selection of real ale pumps. In front of them were beer bar towels that soaked up drops of spilt beer. At the back of the bar the optics sparkled from with light reflected off the mirrors, enticing customers to taste the single malts of Scotland. There was even a small display of snuff, next to a basket of colourfully packaged nuts, Andy felt as though he had travelled back in time, he couldn't help but smile as those glorious days of his youth came flooding back. He ordered a pint of traditional ale, the smooth liquid that tasted even more divine than the whiskey he had become so accustomed to. He sat at the end of the bar, listening to all the chatter and felt a sense of calm as the ale washed away his current problems and replaced them with good time memories.

After listening to much conversation needed another drink, he picked his glass up and signaled to the landlord for a refill. The middle-aged landlord, complete with paunch, quietly asked for the money, but Andy beckoned him to lean forward. Andy quietly requested to buy everyone in the pub a drink, as he had just moved into a house up the road. This brought a look of surprise to the landlord's face, as it had been a long time since someone had done that. He touched his nose, and winked,

"Right you are Sir, leave it to me."

He then went to the bell, used for signaling time for last orders and rang it once."

The whole pub went silent, which was then shattered by the landlords booming voice,

"Right lads and lasses, this gentleman here who I believe has just moved into the big house up the road wants buy us all a drink, one at a time please!"

The way the landlord handled his request brought a smile to Andy's face, as it somehow reminded him of the antics in the Mess hall on his last posting, which always ended looking a right mess!

Naturally the gesture broke the ice, and as the drinks flowed everyone wanted to know the new local man. Andy kept to his new identity which all the patrons believed. He was joking and laughing, something he hadn't done in a long time, it was as if inside the pub, the entire world changed, it had become a friendly place once more. It was sometime later that the bell rang again, signaling last drinks before closing. Andy gave the landlord a fifty-pound note,

"Thanks for a great night now take this and get a taxi for these last few, they're in no shape to walk home let alone drive!"

"Thank you, sir, and may I say it's nice to get a real gent in the manor house for a change, now don't be a stranger. Hardly ever saw the last chap who lived there. He was a politician, never seemed to socialise much ... Looked down on everybody, no time for that sort."

"I know what you mean, best be off. See you soon."

Suddenly Andy's world seemed to come back, leaving the pub all seemed cold and dark once more. As he walked home, he started to analyze himself through the haze of alcohol. Was he in danger of being an alcoholic, or becoming psychotic, he laughed and called out softly into the darkness.

"Well God, you know what I've done in the past. You have my whole family up there, and now I have all this money, is this your way of a joke? If it is, I'm not laughing ... I'm not laughing one bit."

Chapter 5

The sun shone through the bedroom window, alerting Andy that he still had not fixed up the curtains. His head started to swim as he got out of bed, and reminded him of the night before, which brought the inevitable words from his lips, "never again".

He poured a large glass of orange juice from the fridge, to feed his body of the vitamin C the alcohol had destroyed. It was a much welcome taste and felt good.

He switched on the early morning TV News, which added noise to the big empty house. For a brief moment, he imagined movement of a young child eating breakfast at the table in the middle of the Aga heated kitchen. At the kitchen sink he saw his beautiful wife, flicking soap suds at him. It made him feel a lump in his bristled throat and a stabbing pain in his chest, like an old war wound which revisited every so often.

He wiped a tear from his cheek and sat at the empty table. His attention was soon drawn by the TV news of soldiers who had been killed by an explosion in a country that seemed to breathe endless trouble. Monetary aid had been sent in large quantities, yet people still died. It was the type of place Andy hated because it was a place of 'those who have, and those who have not'. It made him even more determined to make those who are in power, pay for the corruption. The phone rang, it was Jimbo with news of the gun, it was good news. It was less than an hour later that Andy arrived at Jimbo's to pick up the weapon and ammunition. It wasn't the make and model he asked for. However, it was a close match and half the price, more than good enough for the job. Jimbo watched as he checked it out in detail. It felt comfortable, light weight and it broke down into a small carry case. Jimbo had chosen well. He looked through a window, stood eight feet from it and took aim at a lamp post further down the road, it felt perfect.

"I need to try it out on your firing range."

Jimbo lead him to it. Andy fired more than dozen rounds, until he was satisfied. He put the rifle into a carry case then turned to Jimbo and gave him an envelope full of cash. Jimbo was curious how Andy had got so much cash and wondered why he needed the gun,

"Mate, I know it's none of my business, but how the hell did you come by so much money, and why the gun . . . You're not killing for money, are you?

"No of course not, I got lucky on the lottery, but that's between you and me." and gave him another envelope of money,

"This is for you, to keep quiet about it."

It contained £200,000 bankers note.

"That too generous bro! But you know me, I would not tell a soul man."

"Of course, I know, I just want you to have the money, sell the shop, retire, whatever. Go and enjoy life!"

"Andy, if you should ever need me, you know where I am." He looked at the cheque then said with a smile, "I've always fancied a little cottage in the Hebrides, away from the rat race to end my days."

Andy knew he could trust him, but to let him in on what he was about to do could sign his death warrant.

After returning home, he was soon back out on the road on his way to the residence of Colin Barnard. His apartment was the penthouse on a three-story block of luxury residences. It was late in the day, and Andy knew that his daily routine meant that he was due home within the next 45 minutes. Opposite was an empty old factory that was planned for renovation. The big sign outside advertised the coming luxury apartments. Whilst studying Barnard, he had decided that this would be the best sniper position, because there was a perfect view from the top of the three-story building. He managed to break in through the back, he used some old packing boxes to lean on, giving him a steady rifle position. He fixed the silencer, rested the rifle on a sock full of sand and waited. The whitewashed window was a good screen, he could see out of, but would be unseen by the occasional passersby. The stories that the young girls had told him of Barnard turned over in his mind, in a way on that convinced him that what he was about to do was right.

Forty-five minutes passed. Barnard was later than usual making Andy just a little impatient. He took out an envelope which contained a type written letter, on its front it read, 'For attention of the POLICE.' Inside with the letter, was the A4 paper signature A.

He placed it on the dusty windowsill. That same moment as Barnard pulled up at the security gates of the apartment building. The gates slowly opened, and he drove in closely followed by the scope of Andy's rifle. Andy calmly waited with his right index finger resting next to the trigger. The car door opened, and Barnard got out, Andy's finger connected with the trigger, as the cross hairs of his rifle scope moved up to Barnards temple. He briefly looked at his own reflection in the door window just Andy's finger gave one squeezed of the trigger. Barnard seemed to freeze as the bullet passed through his temple leaving an eight-foot blood trail, before hitting the lower part of a brick wall. Andy squeezed the trigger once more, this one entering the side of his neck severing the jugular. His supply spurted out all over the roof of the gleaming sports car. He fell backward, his head cracking against the tarmac. The blood pool spread wide and encased his car keys with a key fob of a red devil. This time he didn't put anything in his victims' mouth, the letter said it all.

Andy quickly, but calmly, broke the rifle down and slipped it into the case which made it look like a musical instrument carry case. He made his way out without anyone seeing him leave, to a parallel road where he had left the car.

Back home he sat in front of the TV with a tumbler of scotch waiting for the news. Of course, it may not be on yet, time would tell. It wasn't until the end of the national news that a news flash was broadcasted. It told of how a popular politician Colin Barnard had been killed in a shooting incident. No other details were available, but an update would follow as soon as possible. At the scene the pathologist and forensic team worked to piece together the puzzle and establish where the shots came from.

By 9pm, and five tumblers of scotch later, his tiredness caught up with him and he fell asleep. It was 7am when he woke to the sound of the alarm which told him there was someone at the security gate of his new house, it was Jimbo.

Andy let him in, and he made his way up the short drive. Andy opened the door,

"Shit mate you certainly did win the lottery"

"Well sort of, come in and I'll make coffee."

"OK! Andy be straight with me. Was it you?"

"Was what me?"

"Good God man haven't you been listening to the news. The Politician Colin Barnard has been shot dead. Sounds like a hit to me, the same day you pick up the rifle off me." He paused to look for a reaction, then he continued,

"The young reporter on the local news inferred it was no accident, and I know the guy who found him. His description to me was that of a perfect hit. Temple and jugular for good luck. He's a friend of mine, and this type of news travels at warp speed! They said that his neck was blown out and a bullet hole to the temple, that's clean and accurate, brain matter splattered all over the car and car park." Jimbo paused once more, and look at Andy's lack of emotion, then continued once more.

"The poor bastard that found the mess reacted like most novices do, threw up all over the crime scene, contamination everywhere!"

Only then did Andy show any emotion and quietly laughed with a beaming smile,

"Did he. Poor sod."

Then he signaled with his hand that he was going to making coffee,

"Want one?"

"Yes, but please tell me it wasn't you!"

"OK! It wasn't me!"

Jimbo looked him in the eyes and knew it was a lie, but felt that he should not push the issue . . . not just yet anyway. They both sipped their coffees as the news on the TV told of the murder of Barnard and of his political career. Andy gripped his mug tightly as the reporter told about all of his achievements, his family life , and being a pillar of the community etc, etc. They always do. Jimbocould see by Andy's silence that the story had got under his skin.

"Something tells me that he wasn't all good and that you are not telling me the truth. You know I wouldn't blab mate. If it was you, you must have your reasons."

"Let me show you something."

He pulled out a thick file from a drawer and handed it to him,

"I put this together whilst waiting for the gun. It has all the stories of Barnard, the hidden truth behind the façade. He was guilty of corruption alright. No smoke without fire. Yes, there is fake news out there, but these are the same stories from different sauces. He was scum!"

Jimbo slowly read the file and Andy told him more of his lottery win, then went on to convince him of how he felt about those who were in charge,

"They rule over us, giving us orders, telling us to do this, do that, while they sit back in their chairs and laugh at us all. Remember what we had to do for our Country, the cause. And for what? To come home banged up, shot up and tossed on the scrap heap. In some cases, our guys were dragged through courts with trumped up charges of abusing the enemy. Some survived unscathed, but many don't and it's the same for the civilians, they work their fingers to the bone to see nearly 75% of all they have given to those prats, by direct tax and indirect tax, to squander on rubbish policies and give money away! . . . as though it grows on trees. Even when we die there's inheritance tax, more people than ever get hammered with that one now because of the average value of our homes, they make sure to get as much as possible by the front door and the back. They can't even see that the small man out there earns a tenth of what they deserve, but they still take their pound of flesh. Well I intend to change that!"

"What!...Hold the rich bastards to ransom? Aren't you supposed to have live people to do that?" Jimbo replied with a nervous smile, thinking that Andy had lost the plot.

"Ransom! Yes, but not for money...I intend to take out the bad apples and keep taking them out, until the government changes their polices on how they run this country of ours. It's high time these idiots realized they work for us, not us for them."

That last sentence struck a chord with Jimbo, it now made sense and he could not help but agree,

"You can't do this on your own! We once fought as part of a team, we could again. Haven't got anything else to do, no family to speak of. You and the guys were my family, but most of them never came home. Poor Jeremy, threw himself on that hand grenade to save his team from getting splattered all over the place. It was only days later they died too, and for what, an unjust conflict, built on a lie, by people sitting behind a desk."

Andy pulled out a bottle of scotch and they sat down as they had done many times before under canvas in enemy territory.

***

The following morning Andy woke up in his armchair to see Jimbo flat out on his sofa, snoring. He left him sleeping and went to the shop to get milk and a newspaper. Walking back the realization of last night's conversation meant that there was no going back. Back at the house he made strong coffee and showed Jimbo a small room where he had started to assemble equipment and supplies. Jimbo was impressed, yet still surprised that Andy had taken this course of action. He was unsure of Andy's limits, like knowing when to stop, yet he found himself believing in his mad, wild quest and the ideals of a better world.

Chapter 6

Detective Inspector Harper, known as Harry to his colleagues and friends, chilled out by walking the hill, or riding his bike as he liked to stay fit. He was a slim 45-year-old, with light blue eyes and sandy brown hair. He studied the crime scene photographs after the mornings briefing. It was obviously a professional hit and Barnard did as it seemed have enemies, so why was he killed? Plus, was this connected to the other recent murders?

At the scene, the forensics worked out the direction and angle of the shots. A search of the building opposite was soon in hand and the note left by Andy was found. It was bagged and tagged, and a copy was delivered to Harry's desk. Now the question WHY, was made quite clear. The note read:

Barnard was corrupt and unworthy of a position in Government, all such individuals should perish, and will, as he did.

Judgement Day is about to fall on such scum, until a time that scum, such as he, change.

Today's Government is riddled with vermin, and I am the rat trap. Be sure to let them hear this, so they can steer a better course. Putting the people first, before their own pockets. If these words are not heeded, then hell will follow. For those guilty of crimes against humanity will perish. You will hear from me again.

The letter was signed off by an upside-down A. Plus, the distinctive A4 Signature A. Harry pondered over why it was upside down and the printed one he thought resembled a puzzle. The bar at the bottom of the V when moved up made an inverted A. He was transfixed on it until a young constable brought him a cup of coffee,

"Coffee Sir!"

"Why would someone sign a note with a upside down A? Then this piece of paper with a V that could be an A if you move this bar from the bottom to the middle. It makes an inverted A. What do you think?" Harry asked the young constable.

"Don't know Sir! I thought it was a compass like in those Masonic symbols. It reads almost Biblical. Maybe a Bible punching Mason with a funny handshake."

"Well, yes Thank You Constable for your input, however a Mason! . . . I don't think so, Barnard was a Mason."

Harry tilted his head looking at it,

"The boy may have a point though" he thought.

The phone rang, it was the desk Sergeant who had a Marion Mayer on the phone-line wanting information about the Barnard killing. Harry took the call.

"Detective Harper speaking"

"This is Marion Mayer of the Gazette, could you give me a statement on the death of the politician Barnard, who was found dead next to his residence?"

"We will call a press conference in due course."

49

"Oh! Come on Detective surely you must have something?"

"Yes! You are giving me ear ache." then put the phone down.

***

The Pathologist had just finished his report as Harry opened the door.

"Afternoon Doc, what's the verdict?"

"Well, it's my professional opinion that he's quite dead." he smiled.,

"Killed by a bullet to the temple and a second to the jugular. Instant death."

"Anything else?"

"Yes, the first shot to the temple was either lucky or perfect shot, however considering the second to the jugular was so accurate that it severed the vein and took out most of the windpipe too, I would say the man you are looking for is a crack shot. As for the weapon a very high caliber, professional piece of kit."

Then the Doc touched his arm,

"There is one thing, you remember those pieces of paper removed from the mouths of the recent victims!"

"Yes, what about it?"

"They match the letter left at the scene of this one. You have a serial killer and the letter is a clue to his reason and possible agenda. I think he will kill again, I wouldn't like to be in your shoes. This could get very messy, especially as important people are the targets!"

"Oh! Great! We need to act fast and get results, door knocking time I think!"

A group of constables were sent on a door to door exercise, in search of the answers to many questions. No one had seen anything, Harry knew that the Means, Motive and

Opportunity, would not be uncovered by knocking on doors, but they had to be seen to be busy, as it was a high profile killing. He felt that it had been a professional killer, had covered his tracks well. So, it all depended on forensic evidence and gut feeling, with a little bit of luck. In the forensics lab, no fingerprints were found on the note, nor at the scene. It was assumed that the killer wore gloves. However, the bullet did tell them the type of gun, which was used, and that it was difficult to obtain. It was a very specialized weapon. His mind started to veer towards an ex-military person which ticked all the boxes, except for, who and why?

***

Andy had not told Jimbo of the note he had left at the scene, as he browsed the paper for his next victim. There was a story of a Judge, who had been lenient towards a man convicted of a serious sexual crime towards a 14-year-old girl, which caught his attention. There just below that was another story of a politician who was found to have shares in a company. He sat on the board of directors, and had earned himself a serious amount of money for doing very little, while using his position to ensure the company's growth by securing government contracts. Within the article was a very small paragraph on how disgruntled employees had been complaining about their minimum wage, zero contract hours, unpaid overtime, and only getting 30-minute breaks in a 12-hour shift. Shifts that were 6 till 6 through the day or night, with health and safety rules flaunted constantly. It made his blood boil, that workers in the UK were still abused by the rich and were untouchable. It seemed to echo the working conditions of long ago. It was people like these that made him feel justified in his actions and his plans.

Meanwhile back at the crime scene, Harry took another look at the building where the note had been found, it was a long way opposite the murder site, and where a building had been knocked down in readiness for another apartment complex. There was a car park, making it a long distance to shoot a person so accurately even with using a scope. So many things come into play such as wind direction and moving obstructions. The shooter had patience, steady hand and was a planner, he imagined him waiting for his shot. The thought sent a shudder down his back.

Back at the station the note was opened, and Harry read it again. He turned to his colleague Detective Sergeant Roger Williams, known as Rog. Who had been named after his Grandfather, a man of Jamaican decent, coming to the UK in the 60's. He served his National Service and married a Scottish lass, then settled in the borough of Northfield, Birmingham. Rog was a keen smartly dress young man, who always caught the eye of the ladies.

"No spelling errors and use of words shows a level of intelligence. The hit itself was a clean shot and the crime scene was also clean . . . very professional. So, are we looking at a hitman, terrorist cell, or a nutter?" asked Rog.

"Well, nutter is out, Terrorist cell unlikely, hitman very possible, motive and reason for the hit, possible retribution for his dodgy dealings by the people he's pissed off. So, Rog, the field is wide open, ex-military man, maybe retired with money." replied Harry

"Why Army and why money?" questioned Rog.

"To shoot as good as that, at that distance . . . Sniper training. That caliber of weapon does not come cheap, on the Black Market. It possibly cost more than we earn in a year. Whoever bought that will use it again, and this note proves that, he has a serious agenda. By the looks of things each kill will have the A4 paper with an A or V crap on it. He likes to play games, or just likes to wind us up."

"Why not a she? Ladies are in the Army too!"

"I don't believe a woman would kill in such a way. Killing a perpetrator who has attacked you, family member, or loved one is one thing...this is different. It takes a real callus, cold hearted killer to watch through a rifle scope then see a person's head explode. I doubt very much that it is a woman. Poison is more their game"

Chapter 7

Andy had just finished cleaning the rifle and was surfing the net for information on the next target. Timothy Hyden-White was the Politician he had read about in the newspaper. It seemed unfair that a politician who earned a huge salary could sit on other company boards, earning extra money. Whilst a Soldier or Policeman was not allowed to have second jobs. This situation forced some to moonlight and face dismissal if found out. Hyden-White had 50 employees within the company he owned, most of whom earned below the national wage. It was said that some had wanted to join a union. They soon found themselves unemployed and replaced by agency workers from abroad. He was careful to make sure that the story had not been written by a vindictive reporter, who had a personal axe to grind against Mr. Hyden-White. However, he found many other stories, by other reporters, which all said the same thing. He decided to leave the same note again. A way of embellishing his intentions, but he thought he should play fair, and give them an easier way to contact him as he had no reaction so far. So, he would add that they could place a personal advert in the local paper The Echo, addressed to Mr. A. He got the idea from an old 70's movie that he and his wife used to love watching.

Hyden -White lived in a rural village with a wife whom he treated like a door matt. They had no children, though not through lack of trying, which had left them both bitter.

Andy sat in his car, with a pair of binoculars in his hands, spying on Timothy Hyden-Whites house. He saw him sitting behind a low wall surrounded by a well-kept garden. His wife seemed to be a keen gardener, as she was out each morning by 9am tending to it. Through the kitchen windows at 7.30am she would appear, making breakfast for him and then doing housework until 9 am. After she would then be out in the garden until 4pm.

He felt a sense of sorrow for her as her life although surrounded by a lovely home, seemed empty. At 8.30am Hyden-White left for work and took the same route from Monday to Thursday to his company. By 3.30 he would leave then go to a private address 10 miles away, where he spent 3 hours with another woman.

On Friday and Saturdays from 9.30 till 5pm, he spent in his office just outside Birmingham carrying out his political work surrounded by his staff. Andy could only guess what went on inside, but at 5.30, Hyden-White he did not go home, but went to a private club in the city. Andy now had to decide where he was going to make him meet his maker to pay for the contempt he had for all those around him.

***

That night he planned, with the use of a map the best place for the hit. He decided that the safest place where no one else would be in danger, was in a lane that linked his house to the main road. Traffic had seemed to be very light, with open fields either side and at one point there was a hill, ideal for his positioning to look down on his target as he travelled along the lane.

***

On the morning of the hit, he positioned himself between two trees, leaving a perfect opening for when Hyden-Whites car passed he would have a clear shot. The car came along right on time. Andy waited till the windscreen came just into view in his rifle scope. But then a horse and rider appeared from a gateway and Hyde-White sounded his car horn, making the horse rear up. The rider skillfully brought the horse back under control but was now in the way of a clear shot. The car had stopped but quickly pulled away again. Through the scope Andy could see him cursing the rider, who was riding away in the opposite direction. The shot was now hampered by taller hedges and trees, but up ahead was a gateway which gave Andy one last chance of a clear shot. He covered the trigger as the car approached the gateway. The wind picked up a little a little, so Andy adjusted his aim. In seconds the front of the car came into view through the gateway, then the front wheel, he fired allowing the time delay for the bullet to travel the distance. It shattered the side window and entered Hyden-Whites huge ego, sending it to oblivion. The car shot to the left and up a hedge. Andy checked the rider who was still riding away, oblivious to the crash. Once more Andy calmly packed the rifle away into his 60ltr ruck sack and rode to the car on his dirt bike, he resembled a biker on a camping trip. He screwed up a signature paper up and threw it through the open window of the car. Seconds later another car pulled up and called out to Andy,

"Hi mate, what's happened?"

"Just come across this guy, he's had an accident not sure if he's OK, I've called for the Ambulance they're on their way. I'll stay till they get here, no need for us both to wait."

"OK, I'll get off then as I'm late for work already."

As soon as he was out of sight, Andy left too.

Ten minutes later another car came along and reported the crashed car. Soon afterwards an Ambulance and Police car arrived. They confirmed a shooting, which Harry then attended. In the car with the body was the note. Same note as before with the additional information of a placed advert. Harry and Rog found themselves looking at the most difficult case of their careers, one that had to be solved fast before the shooter struck again.

***

Back at the Police Station Harry had a meeting with his superior, Superintendent Murry, something he always looked forward to, like going to the dentist. Harry tried to convince him that other politicians could be at risk, but his boss believed this to be just another of Harry's hunches, a gut feeling that didn't always prove to be right. However, he had a lot of respect, so he kept an open mind and took all his suggestions on-board but would not act on them just yet. Harry went on to suggest that it would be advisable for all NOT to keep a regular schedule in their daily life, as the hit man had obviously studied these victims closely and knew their every move. They could not offer security for all, so it was down to the individual to be alert. It was obvious to Harry, that the common factor with all victims was character. Those "whiter than white" were safe, those who were not, were fair game and possible targets.

His profile of the hit man was not complete, there were many ex-servicemen. However, they were looking for one who had money, giving him the "means", and records may yet bring up a "motive", and opportunity may mean a retired man, with a grudge against the establishment, who had time on his hands. Rog, started to use the various computer programs to search possible perpetrators, while Harry contacted the MOD for help.

***

Meanwhile Andy was studying the form of a Judge whom he had read about earlier. One who was renowned for letting off the guilty with light sentences, in some cases only a slap on the wrist. He wondered if this behavior was down to their sympathy to fellow twisted people. He tried to source the information from various places to ensure a balanced view. He was very aware that the press could be biased, and sometimes wrong. He was also aware that fake news, at times would be used to destroy people, therefore, he cross referenced all information as much as possible. The evidence which spanned 10 years from various publications was over whelming, added to the fact he had a holiday home in the 'home counties' just an hour's drive away. He decided to go to the Cotswold village to find out which was his house.

***

The next day proved easier than he expected, once he got the address from the electoral roll, he left for the Judges house. It had large motorised iron gates and stone pillars. Behind it was a Cotswold stone gravel drive, with grass lawns either side, that had been rolled to perfection. A security camera was attached to a pole just inside the grounds and pointed towards the gate, and a two-way intercom and a camera built into the brick pillar. Andy drove onto a lay-by and stopped the car, he then pulled out a small drone from the car boot. He set the four-prop drone flying up high then over the perimeter fence. It had a small camera and on the transmitter was a screen. So, the drone was his eye in the sky. The drone hovered, and checked all round. It flew to the front door then the lower windows one by one and checked out security. Through each window he could see motion sensors and alarms. He noticed the lack of a woman's touch, no frills, or family photos on the fireplace. The rooms were functional, and extremely neat. He wondered about the wife, maybe she never came here? When the drone got to the last corner of the house a face suddenly filled the screen. It was the gardener who tried to swipe at it,

"Bloody boys and their toys! Piss-off you peeping Tom"

Andy pulled it back and it shot upwards to roof height where it hovered and did a panoramic view of the grounds, and the tall fencing which surrounded them. He brought the drone back to the car and quickly put it back in the boot.

***

Driving back, he thought about the Judges wife, he reasoned that the Judge was the mark and not his wife. Why should he ruin her future life by killing him in her home? So, it was going to be hit while the Judge drove from, or back to the house.

***

Back home he watched the film footage that he had taken with his dash cam of the road which lead to the Judges house.

There was a problem, the distance from the village to the house was a quarter of a mile, and people seemed to walk their dogs there at various times of the day. A horse-riding school further down this road also used it a lot. All adding to possible witnesses, but more importantly innocent people could be put in danger.

A map showed two roads leaving the village, both of which the Judge could use, so for the next two weeks he studied his movements with interest, and he found that he favoured the straightest road, where he always travelled on his own. It had no blind bends that could be used as target points, but the one he used to travel at speed made him a more difficult target. He thought of ways to slow him down or stop him. A farm tractor coming out of one of the many field gates could prove to be the perfect remedy. He used his drone to search out a vehicle from a nearby farm whilst he sat in his car in a lay by. There was a track which left the farm and led to a field with a gate, less than quarter of a mile away. In the farmyard, were two tractors and an old Land Rover series 2, which looked as though it was only used to ferry straw bales and cattle feed around the various fields. Fresh mud on its wheels confirmed it was a runner and Andy knew it would be easy to hotwire if required. The only other problem was a Border Collie who seemed to roam free around the farmyard.

On the day that the Judge was to die he drove at a steady pace listening to The Two Cello's, playing their rendition of Thunderstruck, a piece that is almost gave a macabre, match his mood. He knew the Judge was due to go back to the house, so he went to the farm which seemed to be very quiet. The tractors that had been there were gone, which indicated that the farm hands were all out in the fields. To his delight the keys to the Land Rover were in the ignition, however, his stealthy approach had been spotted by the Border Collie who, like all dogs, had an amazing sense of smell. He barked a few times then he gradually made his way towards Andy, and growled and when he got to him, he had a sniff. He could smell food! Andy removed from his backpack his secret weapon, dog food which was already in a plastic dish covered in cling film which he removed, which delighted the dog. He patted the Collie, placed the food down and the dog got stuck in. Andy slowly got in the Land Rover and drove away down the track. At the gate, he stood and waited with the engine ticking over as he used binoculars to watch for the Judge. He didn't have to wait long, he jumped back in the Land Rover and pulled out just as the Judge got to him. The Judge braked hard. Andy got out of the Land Rover with a pistol with a silencer which he concealed, tucked in the back of his jeans. He walked up to the car and gestured for him to wind down the window and then Andy smiled,

"Sorry Judge!"

"You know me? I'm sorry but I don't recognise you!" replied the Judge.

"No judge, we've never met. I am here to sentence you for all the CRAP judgements you have made over the years, letting scum get away with murder, rape and generally not being very nice people . . ."

"How dare you, get out of my way!" the Judge growled.

"No Judge, this is your judgment day."

In a split second the thud of a bullet leaving the silencer was the last sound the judge heard. His intelligence and arrogance decorated the passenger seat and door. Andy put an envelope on the Judges lap and screwed up a A4 signature and pushed it into the judge's mouth. Then he quickly returned to the farm with the Land Rover, he patted the Collie as he left in a calm manner as he removed the rubber gloves he was wearing.

It was only 10 minutes later that the judge was found, and another 20 minutes until Detective Inspector Harry Harper and Detective Roger Williams arrived on the scene. The familiar envelope was bagged for Forensics, and Harry started to scan the area.

The pathologist was on site quickly and soon found the signature in the Judges mouth. He pointed it out to Harry and Roger who instantly started to panic at the speed that the bodies had now turning up, they franticly looked around for any clue of where the shooter had disappeared.

"Rog look at this!" On the road in front of the car was the dry dirt tyre tracks of the Land Rover.

"Looks like these tracks come out, then go back into the field as if a vehicle was used to stop this one. Odds on it's a Land Rover, recognise the tread pattern, I had an LWB 12 seat Safari with all the kit, years ago, loved it."

"Why sell it then?"

"Kids came along, needed something cheaper! Anyway, I digress. You and I are taking a walk so bring a radio. I am hoping that somewhere up here is the offending Land Rover with heaps of forensics inside."

They followed the tracks right up to the Land Rover, which resulted in getting their nice shoes and suits caked in dirt. It was the open back pick-up type with a tatty canvas cover. Rog attempted to look inside it, and the Border Collie leapt forward barking which sent Rog falling backwards onto the ground. He got up frantically and dusted off the dirt. Harry offered the Collie a closed fist,

"It's alright boy, here smell my hand." and gradually the Collie let him stroke him.

"Rog, with all the aftershave you wear, I'd be surprised he can smell the real you."

"Oh! Very funny, Harry." he said as he took Harry's offer of a helping hand up.

Harry checked the cab but found nothing. Rog tried to inspect the back and make friends with the dog, he then spotted something on the ground about 20 feet away. He walked over to it, and took out an evidence bag, picked it up and bagged it. Harry saw him and called out,

"I'd like SOCO to look over it, but it's filthy in there, I won't hold my breath. What's that you got there?"

"Rubber glove, like we use to collect evidence, and I doubt these are the farmers, they tend to use heavy weight stuff, and this one still feels fresh. Not been out in the sun for too long."

"Get it to Forensics, you never know. Shit, we need some luck on this one, now he's bumping off Judges. Although to be fair, this wanker of a Judge let off several of my cases with a slap on the wrist! Most re-offended within weeks." he paused and looked into Rogers eyes,

"My God, this guy is willing to kill anyone high ranking, with a dodgy past, or crooked smile. He's like a Robin Hood, giving out Justice instead of money. Maybe he sees himself as an avenging angel." He then turned to walk back along the track and to the car.

"That's a very profound profile! So, you see this guy as a hit man, or a special forces guy sent by God." asked Roger.

Harry turned and pointed at Rog, "This is why you are a Detective, we need to check on the special forces. Politicians sent them to illegal wars where they must have seen plenty of their guys die, due to lack of funding and equipment. That's been banged around the media a few times. Assassination and planning like this is second nature to him. Rog, I think our list of suspects is getting smaller. We need to nail him before he gets another."

It was just at this point the farmer turned up with his tractor and Harry went on to explain what had happened. He checked that the Land Rover was his, and that it would have to be processed.

"Oh! Yes, one other thing. Do you use thin rubber gloves like mine?" holding his pair in the air,

"No, we don't, those thin things wouldn't last seconds on farm."

"Well again, thank you for your cooperation."

As they got the evidence to forensics Andy was already planning another hit and searching for a target.

***

The media was starting to show an interest, namely Marion Mayer, a glamorous brunette who used her looks and charm to get the best stories. She rang Harry for any comments, but he replied that no he could not give her anything, but a news release would soon be forthcoming.

Harry and Rog made enquiries with the MOD regarding retired special forces, and spoke to a Colonel who was Adjutant at the Special Forces camp, but this had to go through so many channels and red tape that a quick result was looking unlikely. Harry asked if fingers print record were carried for all personnel, to which the reply was "no"!

***

That night Andy slept restlessly; when he did fall into a deep sleep the nightmares started, visions of fallen comrades, deafening explosions, flying dirt that stung his face, choking smoke and body parts covered the ground releasing a smell that hung in the air, on your clothes, in your nostrils. No matter how many times he washed in the dirty puddle, the blood would not leave his hands. A head with no body was calling to him, but he could not get off his knees. A mist would form, and he found himself floating into another nightmare with his children and his wife, who were playing on swings, surrounded by green grass. The sunshine disappeared, he looked up to the dark clouds which covered the sun. He looks back to his family covered in blood, calling for him, but the faster he ran in the dream the further the distance became. He woke up in a cold sweat, the bed sheets soaked and his heart pounding.

***

In the morning Jimbo telephoned and asked how he was, and whether he needed anything,

"No, I'm fine mate, but may call on you for a favour soon."

"Andy, I know it's none of my business, and I might be wrong, but this latest hit on the Judge ... was it you?"

"That's right ... it's not your business!"

***

Two hours later Andy was still looking at the news on the internet and he had finally found another target. Meanwhile Harry received news from Forensics, so he called in to see them,

"So, what do you have for me?"

"The Land Rover was a dead end, however, the rubber glove proved interesting. I managed to pull a print off the inside of it. Only one finger was good enough as the others were smudged."

"Any hits on the print."

"This isn't TV or the Movies Harry, it takes time, but what we do have; and I think you forgot about is the sealed note."

"Same as the other I assume?"

"No, it's not. I am sure it's the same person, because of the M.O. but it also speaks volumes on his state of mind."

Harry looked intrigued and read out loud the note which was in a plastic bag.

"Any DNA on the envelope?"

"No, he used a self-adhesive envelope. He is, thorough but the glove may be his first mistake! Probably dropped in error, otherwise both gloves would have been discarded. Fingers crossed!"

"Signed it 'A' again. What's that stand for. Alpha, Avenger, or Asshole!"

"Just read it Harry!"

"*He will wipe away every tear from their eyes and Death shall be no more, neither shall be mourning, nor crying, nor pain anymore, for the former things have passed away. Revelation 21.4. Vengeance will be mine.*"

He paused as a chill went down his spine,

"He's quoting the Bible, book of Revelations. He does see himself as an avenging angel, one that doesn't fear death. That's all I need ... a Special Forces Vet hell bent on revenge on the establishment. He's so not scared, he spends time placing notes for us to find and even putting one in the victims mouth. Anybody else would be running, getting out of there! But not our guy! That's what frightens me the most. He either doesn't care, or he sees himself invincible."

"Why do you think Special Forces ... You mean SAS." Ask the Doc

"It's a hunch, a gut feeling and this one has found religion! He even wants us to place an ad in the personal column of the local paper, The Echo, giving some sort of reply to his demands ... Bloody hell, I need a stiff drink!"

The Doc continued,

"You could be right, the state of the criminal mind is a hobby of mine, so last night I looked up all the deaths so far, and not one has a clean record. In fact, he has picked all those that are in the media constantly with bad press."

Harry instantly dialed Rog on his mobile,

"Rog, drop whatever you're doing and go on the net, look up news and bad press on Politicians and Judges. See if any dead bodies come up, then look for those still living, and one of them could be the next target. I know it's a needle in a haystack, but until a hit on the fingerprint comes up, this is all we've got. Give priority to those living within the home counties, as I think he is based here, and will not want to spread himself too thinly. Unless he's got help, if so, God help us!"

Chapter 8

Andy was in his garage fixing bull bars to his Range Rover as Jimbo arrived, on a bright, but chilly morning. Andy buzzed him through the security gates and Jimbo admired the classic Range Rover 3.5 Auto. It wouldn't win prizes for being immaculate, but the engine was strong and sound, as was the chassis.

"Nice bit of kit mate, but why the extras. You going to ram something, or somebody? Come on bro! I know it's you and why you're doing it. But, shit Mate, we both know you never do missions on your own, and I am sick with the crap we put up with from the establishment. My life is crap, I want to live again . . . I'm dying anyway!"

"Dying! What do you mean?"

"It's terminal brought it back from Iraq they reckon. A number of the guys developed it. I can have treatment and lose my hair. Live a few months extra but get weaker, not even have a hard on! Live in hospital until the bitter end . . . Life's a bitch, let me die as the lord intended but, I want to go out with a bang! I won't let you down. I have no family, no one will miss me when I'm gone! I want to feel alive once more, now I'm existing, but not living."

His voice almost seemed to plead with Andy,

"I know you wouldn't, but the risks are high. This isn't Queen & Country!"

"I know it's for justice of the common man . . . and woman! Besides I met the Queen once, and I'm bloody sure she hates crooks as much as we do. Crooked Government makes her look bad!"

Andy smiled, at the thought that he wasn't alone feeling the way he did."

***

Back at the Police Station, there was still no news on the finger print.

"Why can't it be like on TV. Scan the print and seconds later you've got your man. Pop out with some hot looking female detective, quick arrest then back to some fancy wine bar for cocktails. What do I get, dab's done via snail mail, a male detective who's a neat freak, a pub that sells flat beer with and packets made from half a potato?" moaned Harry.

"Who's a neat freak? I just care about my appearance, keeping fit, and losing a few pounds wouldn't go amiss on you!" smirked Rog.

"Oh! Shut up! Let's go back to doing the computers and go through as many files as we can. Something might come up."

Harry's mobile went off, it was Marion Mayer,

"Hello Harry, look I know you said you had nothing, but can I just have a chat, off the record, honestly." She pleaded.

"Yes OK. I can give you 5 minutes when you get here!" replied Harry.

"I'm already here in reception!" she said in a perky voice!

He sighed as he put the phone down, "It's going to be an awkward day. I know it is!" Then he went to collect her from reception then took her to an empty room,

"Look Marion, I don't want to mess you about but, this case is extremely difficult. By the way, print any of this and I will make your life hell! You will never work as a reporter again."

"Wow! It must be a hush, hush one then. Hold on don't tell me someone is going around bumping off all the bent big-wigs he can get his hands on!" then laughed. But Harry looked at Rog and both looked back at her, with serious faces.

"Oh! My God! You are not serious!" with a wry smile, not knowing whether to laugh or cry.

"Marion, it is possible you can help us but on one condition, you cannot tell anyone what so ever, of what you know, and I really mean this. In return, you will get the scoop of the century, making Jack the Ripper look like Mary Poppins. This story will be talked about for decades and you will be the reporter people will turn to, because there will not be News Releases like on other cases. Giving you plenty of time to report it well, maybe even write a book!"

"That big, OK, shake on it. What do you want from me?"

"Research accidents, where family members have died where the husband is a soldier. We also need to place an ad in the personal column, but your paper must not know where it's come from. No one, but no one, knows about this. You must keep it to yourself."

"Stop it, your worrying me now, so this guy's good?"

"I've been a copper for a long time and in that time, I have never known a case like this. Not even those I've read about. I can't say any more now, but here is my card, on the back are my personal numbers. Ring me, don't care what time of day it is if you have a problem, you call me."

***

Marion left unsettled and scared but went straight back to the office, she sat at her desk and carried out searches using the information she had, which wasn't much. Accident and deaths of family members with the father or family member being military personal. She did a search of stories covered over the past six years. Then she cross referenced that list with people living in a 50-mile radius. Harry felt it had a bearing on the crime sites. The list was reducing, but still nearly 100. The next day she carried on with the searches, which were taking longer than she thought. As she had to go through each one in some detail. That night Marion slept uneasy, and tossed and turned with the knowledge that bounced around in her head.

She was not the only one, as the person that they were searching for, Andy, also had yet another long night of bad dreams.

The next day Andy carried on with the research of his next target, while Marion carried on cross referencing her media stories. The last search she tried were stories from the last two years, and five stories came up which she printed off.

***

It was four in the afternoon when she called Harry to form him of her lists. In the room, she placed out the stories that spanned 6 years. Both Harry and Rog were in shock at the amount, Harry felt despondent at the thought of many weeks it would take to checking each one out. In the meantime, people were dying. Then she put the five full stories down, that went back 2 years. Harry and Rog took a keen interest and

71

studied each in turn. The first story was of a retired 65-year-old soldier of the Royal Signals who lost his wife in a car crash. Harry put it to one side,

"Too old, a man of that age would not go off the rails. A communications man is hardly a hardened killer, even if they do basic training, it's just that. Basic! Our man is a trained killer, planner, expert in most things of that nature ... I still put money on a Special Forces vet."

The second was a retired Military Surgeon, who lost his wife in a house fire,

"He saves lives, not take them."

The third was a retired Royal Engineer who had lost his wife on a skiing holiday,

"Another no go! ... It doesn't gel that was an accident. He builds things, not tear them down."

The fourth was a retired paymaster, a local celebrity who raised much for charities. He had lost his elderly wife, whilst with other pensioners, who were on an annual outing in a mini bus accident.

"Zimmer frame vigilante just doesn't work for me. Go ahead punk make my ... what day is it sonny? Plus, the fact it was an accident, no one to blame."

Harry slid it to one side,

"Again no, none of these fit. Maybe I am barking up the wrong tree, I suppose thinking a retired soldier would do such a thing, is a bit much. I suppose there may be such a thing as a really talented amateur!"

The fifth was of a younger soldier who was decorated for his involvement with the Parachute Regiment, during a campaign who lived just outside Birmingham. Originally from Hereford in the home counties. This man lost his wife and daughter who had been involved in a hit and run. They were hit by a young driver who was later arrested and charged with drink/driving, and killing whilst driving without due care and attention. A young boy was also seriously hurt, resulting in him being in a coma. The young boy lost his battle earlier this year, when asked, Mr. A McIntosh, father of the two children and husband to the young woman replied,

"I hope he gets what he deserves, and ,with luck God will not forgive this scum." Mr. David Conway served 18 months.

Harry had a feeling this one may, be the one, and needed to be looked at in detail,

"He was from Hereford, what's the betting he was SAS, many from the Para's were selected for them. Young family, so he is young possibly 40's. Lost all his family to a piss head driver, who is out after 6 years. That would make many people pissed off, and make a SAS veteran, crack! let's face it, someone like that sees many of his mates killed. Back to civvy street, to see your wife and kids killed in such a way . . . not good."

Rog agreed but pointed out,

"It's only him if the fingerprint fits!"

"So, we find him and get one."

***

The following day both Harry and Rog gathered what information they had on Andy there wasn't a huge amount other than that which Marion had found, giving her many Brownie points with Harry, who recapped with Roger their aim,

"I don't have to tell you that there is, 'Motive, Opportunity and Means' to all crimes. If Mr. Andy McIntosh is our man, then these must be proven, paramount for a court case.

1. <u>Motive</u>, he saw many colleagues die in the field, may be on missions he thought were pointless. Then there is the straw that broke the camel's back, to lose his entire family, wife and

two kids, to a drunk punk who drove off and left them to die. Son survived but died later . . . a vegetable. Prat of a Judge gives the punk a feeble sentence. Maybe this is something he has done many times. A sizeable number of them our cases, if you remember. Now I call that bloody good motive.

2. <u>Opportunity</u>, he's retired, but we need to find out if he's working at all. If not, then he has ample opportunity.

3. <u>Means</u>, we know roughly the type of gun used. They are not cheap, and on the Black Market can be a small mortgage. So, we must find out about his finances. So, let's get to work, and I'll ask Marion if she could find possible targets via the various medias that are within in a 50-mile radius. I know he could go out of that area, but we need a starting point."

"OK, I'll get us some coffee, and look into his finances."

Meanwhile Andy was doing his own sourcing of the next target. While the minutes ticked by, Harry built a profile on Andy, they were also getting closer to yet another dead body. He had always believed in a theory that the EU was run by a corrupt group of none elected individuals, with the intent of creating a super state, to absorb each country's wealth. All under one roof, one ruling court and one undemocratic governing body. A world with a new super class system would prevail, and the divide between them and the working class, would widen. This type of thing had happened so many times. Empires came and went, and never worked, as they grew too large. Mongol, Roman, British and USSR, maybe wearing different disguises, but underneath they were basically the same.

To effectively stop them was not a one-man job, but Rome wasn't built in a day. So, for now Andy would concentrate on the corruption at home. He noticed that the news on such stories was getting thin in the media, and wondered if his actions were having some desired effect. In the local Echo Newspaper, he turned to the personal column and found the message sent by Harry,

"Mr. A, love to chat to you regarding our problem. Regards Harry," followed by his mobile number. Andy liked the dark humour of calling it a 'Problem',

"Problem . . . Problem! My God Harry, I've only just started."

He got up from his desk to make himself a mug of coffee. He put coffee in the mug and seeing that he was almost out of it, he felt in his pockets for cash, and pulled a rubber glove that he had used to sentence the Judge. He put his hand back in to find the matching one, but it wasn't there. He went to the garage and checked the car. It wasn't there either, so he walked the route from there to the house and around the house to see if it was dropped anywhere. Nothing. Now he was concerned, in the combat fields forensics it was not a huge issue, but now it was. He was aware, after seeing a program that it was possible to retrieve a finger print from the inside of a glove. So, he thought there's a small chance they could, and that was only if they found it. He could not let it cloud his future actions, and had to proceed, but keep it in ,mind to be more thorough on his future missions. He took his coffee back to his desk and carried on looking for the next target. He looked back at the personal advert and decided to call Harry later that day, just after he had chosen a target. He went to page two, while a news program opened on the computer. On the page was a dozen stories but only one political and that was not bad. Page after page, but nothing jumped out at him. His mind kept wondering back to the missing glove. Then he had an idea of how to defuse the situation. He rang Jimbo and asked him to call round.

When he arrived, Andy told him of his idea to do two hits at once,

"You see Jimbo, they may have a print of mine from the inside of the rubber glove. So, if two hits happen at once, it just might let them think that there's more than one, a group, a possible terrorist cell."

"Possible, but shouldn't worry too much mate, taking the things off would smudge any prints left inside." Assured Jimbo.

"True!" nodded Andy.

"Who was your next target then?"

He then went on to show Jimbo the paper and internet possibilities,

"In the paper, there is nothing really of worth, but on the internet news two caught my eye."

He opened a page showing an article of a County Councilor accused of rigging planning bills in favour of a company, of which he sat on the board. It was not the first time he had been accused, but this time he resigned from his position due to pressure. However, he moved straight into another high paid job working for a large global company, which in it self, had a dubious history of dodgy dealings. The other one was of a Lawyer who for the past 20 years had been very successful at getting people off various offences such as drink driving, to murder. Andy knew that even crooks needed a fair trial but making hideous amounts of money from other people's heart-breaking events seemed sickening.

So, he went to work on making two dossiers on the targets, Councilor David Butterworth, and Lawyer, Antony John-Thomas. Meanwhile Jimbo started making two bombs and also assembled a remote-control model plane, a Pulse Jet model plane for propulsion, and to carry the small explosive device. It was quite a large delta shaped plane of which he had to harden the nose tip without altering the weight too much. He fashioned a nose cone from aluminum to a point. With it, a launch pad that pointed 35 degrees into the air, which could be attached to a roof rack, to launch the jet. Remote clamps would hold it in place while the engine was started up and then released when launched.

***

It was late in the afternoon and Harry and Roger found some more details on Andy, namely his length of service in the Army, the name of company he started up afterwards, and how long it's been since he last worked, which was two years. This drew Harry to the conclusion that two years could easily eat away at savings, meaning that he may not have the 'Means' to afford such a weapon that was used. They assumed that any money gained from leaving the Army would have gone into the security company, however, they still had to confirm his finances.

Marion, however, had more luck. She thought, as she searched for up-to-date news of possible targets, that fell into the category. There were four that had recently hit the head-lines, one of which was Councilor David Butterworth. A man she had interviewed once at his office. She remembered that he came from behind his desk and sat a short distance in front of her so he could get a better view of her legs. She had worn a black off the knee bodycon. It was sexy, but she wore it as it was comfortable, and smart, as it stretched nicely when sat at her desk. Now it was showing her curvaceous size 12 body off to perfection, which made Butterworth almost drool. At this, Marion very unsettled, and she tried to pull the hem fur-ther down, but this just made it worse as it sprang back, to reveal more, 'nearly black pantyhose' and athletic thighs. He was obviously aroused, this made Marion want to heave, as she asked more questions regarding the Councils plans and his political views on Central Government. She knew that her appearance often made men like him talk and show off their power and their male ego, which made great news. Near the end he leaned forward to touch her knee, and she stood up,

"Oh! Gosh! I was so engrossed I forgot the time," as she checked her watch.

"I have another appointment I must not miss."

"Well, my dear, maybe we could carry on this chat one evening this week?"

"Yes, I will call you."

That was some months ago! But the memories still gave her the chills. He was slimy, and her in-depth research found him to be the giver and acceptor of many bribes. She was sure corruption was his mistress and the only person he cared about was the man in the mirror. Yes, he could be a target.

***

Andy had been following Anthony John-Thomas, the Lawyer and Jimbo following Butterworth, both made detailed reports on their movements and habits. John-Thomas drove the same route every day, but he also took a morning jog along the lanes, near his country house, making him an easy target.

Butterworth drove the same route also every day, but on busy main roads except one. It was a rat run, used by those who knew it as a way of avoiding traffic between two major roads. Fields either side, making it seem the perfect spot for a hit. It was decided that to use the Pulse jet there, the only disadvantage was the nose it created, however, if Jimbo flew it from a good vantage point that was concealed then the bomb laden plane could hit its target with ease. Jimbo had flown drones many times, but this flew faster and could carry the weight of explosives. He felt sure that it wouldn't be a problem. But for additional help he fitted a small camera underneath, to give him a bird's eye view.

Marion met Harry and told him of her concerns about Butterworth, so Harry decided that tailing Butterworth for the next week would be worth it.

***

Later that day Andy called the number from the advert left in the personal adds in the paper and spoke to Harry,

"I will make this quick as I know you will be trying to trace this call. My demands for policy change and ridding the Government, Councils and Law Departments of self-centered, corrupt scum must be done. If not, more WILL die!

I have shown you what I am capable of, and unless I see you are taking this seriously by making an announcement on TONIGHT'S local TV News, then two more will die tomorrow."

"TONIGHT! TWO? Tomorrow! I need more time, I can't organise that at this stage!"

"What's the value of life Harry?"

"A lot, you can appreciate that . . . surely!" Harry replied.

"Yes, I do Harry, that is why I am doing this. Many have died because of scum like this not giving a SHIT about people, only their pockets. You had best get a move on Harry, because time is running out for your task, and for two people who may die tomorrow." The phone went dead. Harry started making frantic phone calls. His superior said,

"Harry the guys a crank and another thing, how is he going to kill two? Be in two places at once! Look I'm in the middle of a dinner with some important people and Councilor David Butterworth wants me, I'm going to have to go, I will speak with you tomorrow."

"Butterworth! He could be a target Sir!"

"Detective Inspector Harris, Councilor Butterworth is fine and here, surrounded by lots of people, quite safe."

"Sir, the hit will be tomorrow unless we get something on tonight's local TV News."

"Inspector, do you honestly believe I can, or will, be able to organise something like that on the ravings of an idiot. Its 5pm! The news is on in an hour! Look I can understand your worry, but honestly the man is a crank. How do you know it was him that called you and not another crank, or even kids? Placing an add like that was not a clever idea."

"But Sir people have died already because of this crank!"

"I'm sorry Inspector I have to go, this is a very special fund raiser. We will speak tomorrow; the film crew have just arrived, I have to speak with them."

So, Harry rang Butterworth's office and left a message on his answer service telling him to be careful and alter his daily routine. He then rang the TV News office and told them he needed to put out an announcement,

"I am sorry Sir, but the schedule is full for tonight. Too late to do any changes now. However, we could give you a slot tomorrow night, we will have a film crew available then."

"But this is urgent!"

"Always is, I am afraid, but you see the last film crew that was available was called out to cover a Fund Raiser that's being filmed live. In fact, it was Councilor Butterworth who called us out. I have to go … sorry, but like I say we can help you tomorrow."

Harry sat in his chair open mouthed, the whole situation had become surreal. He called Roger and brought him up to speed. He, in turn, spoke to a friend and colleague who served on the arms response unit and asked if he could be ready the following day to be called at a moment's notice. He replied,

"No problem, any chance you know where, whatever it is may happen."

"Um! Within a 50-mile radius ... we think!"

"Well, we like a challenge, that's over an hour's drive with the lights on. Thanks a bunch Roger! Beers on you then."

***

In the morning, Jimbo took Andy's Land Rover with the plane and launching platform in the back. He had fitted false plates and grounded the chassis numbers away, so that the vehicle could not be traced, just in case! Andy used his off-road motorbike to meet up with John-Thomas, while Harry and Rog waited for Butterworth to appear from his house.

Meanwhile, Marion was writing a report on the very Fund Raiser that Butterworth was at, she had attended, but only stayed long enough to get a few picture, quotes and information. Then she was off home, to soak in a bath sipping at a lightly chilled glass of white wine.

***

Andy waited with a pistol and silencer concealed under his jacket. Then John-Thomas came out of his house for his morning 2-mile jog. As he ran, Andy watched then slowly pulled away as John -Thomas disappeared around a bend some distance ahead. Andy passed him on the muddy lane and soon as he cleared a bend stopped. Lay the motorbike down then pretended to be unconscious and waited. John-Thomas came around the bend and saw Andy on the floor and ran to him,

"You alright?" Andy pretended to come around.

"Yes, I must have slid in all the mud."

"I'm a lawyer, you could sue for this you know. Of-course there are fees, but I could promise you a settlement. Take the farmer for all he's got, after he left the lane in such a state."

"I'm glad to say that!"

"Yes, there is big money to be earned from such situations."

"Makes my job easier."

"What's that then." Andy produced the weapon with silencer.

"Executioner." John-Thomas flew back and hit the ground with a thud, as the bullet left a hole between the surprised wide-open eyes. Blood trickled out and filled his eye socket, while the hole at the back of his head spewed blood onto the road.

Andy got up quickly, put the signature paper in his mouth then rode off in the direction of where Jimbo was to meet his target.

Jimbo had just finished erecting the launch platform on the ground and used tent pegs to secure it. He placed the plane with the explosives built into the body with a device to make it explode on impact. There was also a small metal tube inside containing a rolled-up signature sheet inside it. Through binoculars he saw Butterworth's distinctive classic red Jaguar series 3, turn into the clear road. The plane took off at speed and Jimbo had it flying a circuit until Butterworth came within range. Using the camera on the plane gave him an amazing view, which made him feel like a bird. The pulse jet could be heard by the houses just down the road, but it flew so fast, and as it the size of a coffee table, was not easily seen in the sky. Then the plane swooped down heading for the Jag. Jimbo's view with the plane's camera was very clear as the plane and headed for the Jag. Butterworth was listening to Garry Glitter on his audio system with the volume up, he was unable to hear the oncoming buzz of the jet. Jimbo brought the plane down at a 35% angle aiming at the windscreen. By the time he saw it, it was too late. The Pulse Jet punctured through the windscreen like an armour piercing rocket. The explosion was spectacular and Jimbo instantly jumped back in the Land Rover, and drove off, with dirt spraying in all directions, to the exit as planned. But he hadn't noticed, that Harry and Roger were in a car following, and saw the explosion,

"BLOODY HELL! What was that?" shouted Harry.

"Something hit the car and exploded!"

"What and from where?"

"Land Rover at 3 o'clock, in the field, driving like stink. Could be our man!"

Rog called the Armed Response Unit, who with lights and sirens screaming, made their way to the scene.

Harry blocked the field entrance with his car and Jimbo swerved around and headed to the other at the end of the field, churning up grass in all directions. Rog radioed, telling the Unit of the Land Rovers course. They were not going to be there on time, so Harry did a 3-point turn and with siren and lights going, shot to the other exit. When they got there, Jimbo had already turned and was heading back to the original exit. Rog Radioed the Unit again to tell them.

"OK. You get back to that exit and we will take the one you're at now. We're are less than one minute away."

Harry got back to the road which lead to the original exit, but Jimbo was already coming out and heading for them. He braked hard and started going back the other way which now was blocked by Butterworth's burning wreck, completely blocking the road, so he turned back into the field clipping the hedge. He raced to the other exist only to meet the armed response unit blocking it. Now both exits were blocked, and a helicopter above had joined in the chase. Jimbo was stuck, but he had a surprise up his sleeve. The Police used a loud haler to call him. It was Harry,

"Mr. A. It is hopeless we have armed Police, please get out of the vehicle and lie face down."

Jimbo called Andy with his mobile phone, Andy pulled over and answered his call,

"Jimbo, how's it going?"

"Mission completed in spectacular style, but Andy I'm caught mate, no way out, but I'm going to give you a way out though! They think I am you. I rigged your motor with the good stuff, I won't feel a thing. I am well away from the coppers and anyone else, no one else will be hurt. Like I told you over a beer, I want to go out with a bang. When I do, they will think you are dead. I am dying anyway, this way I can give my best mate a gift, the chance to walk away and start again, because Mr. A' dies with me . . . and Andy, do yourself a favour go and live my dream in the Hebrides, wear a kilt and give your bollocks an airing! Forget these bastards."

"Jimbo, don't do this . . . please. You're the only close friend I have."

"True, but now I will be even closer. Doc's didn't give me long to live anyway. I don't want to die riddled with cancer. I've always had your back mate, no more than now. Take care bro!"

Harry was still waiting for a response,

"Mr. A. The situation is hopeless." then there was a huge explosion and fire ball.

The Police looked on in shock, and disbelief, Andy for the first time got off his bike, sat on the curb and cried.

Chapter 9

At the Police Station Harry and Roger were under the impression it was all over until the finger print result came through from forensics,

"We have a confirmation on that finger print in the rubber glove, and we sent out a member of the team to confirm it."

"And?"

"It belonged to the farmer's son whose old Land Rover was used on the shooting. He found it on the floor and used it when disposing of a dead rat on the farm."

"OK, thanks."

"Well that settles it Rog. The print belonged to the farmer's son who had used it after the event, to get rid a flee bitten rat, and our rat was blown up in the Landy"

"Sorry Harry, but a confirmed killing identical to the others of a Lawyer just come through."

"Maybe he did that before blowing himself and Butterworth up."

"Not according to the Doc, he thinks it's doubtful, because the body was still really warm when found, dead no more than 30 minutes, and it was 45 miles away at the time, that's a good hour drive at least maybe more!"

Harry tried to convince himself that the Doc and Rog were wrong.

"Well he can't be in two places at once, unless there have always been two of them. Then we have to ask is there more than one killer, why is it when I think we are on top of this, the rug gets pulled."

The phone rang, it was forensics, to say they had found a metal tube in the car wreckage that had been in the model flying bomb. Inside was the signature sheet, although damaged and a little burnt, it was defiantly genuine.

Then the phone went again, it was Superintendent Murray whom he had spoken to the previous night,

"I am sorry Harry, but now be rest assured that it's all over eh!"

"Well, no we can't sir, we believe he may not be dead. There is a chance that he had an accomplice."

"WHAT! If he calls, record it! and keep me informed. I don't fucking care what time of day or night it is, you call me. Next time he wants an answer from us via the media, I will make sure it happens. From now on Harry, you have no other work cases other than this. You want extra coppers with you . . . you, just pick up the phone. This takes priority over everything else. Now I need Aspirin." Announced Murray

"Thank you, sir."

Then he rang off,

"Roger my dear fellow. I do believe I just had my ass kissed. Whatever we want, or need anything, we have it from the powers on high! Probably because it's the powers on high, that are the targets!" he sniggered.

Marion phoned after hearing the news from her contacts,

"Harry! Hi. Heard the news! Is it true . . . it's over?"

"No! Possibly not. The finger print was ruled out and the two killings this morning seem to make it near impossible for him to have committed both murders, this of course is off the record, as our agreement is still on!" replied Harry.

"What about the info I gave you on that guy, Andy McIntosh?"

"We have no evidence. We are still waiting on his personal information, because . . . well let's leave it there for now." Said Harry.

"OK. I was right on the target though! So, I will see if I predict again?" she gleefully replied.

"Yes please. If it wasn't for you then we would have been none the wiser. So please keep it up and like I said, when the case is over, the news scoop is yours."

Once again on the premise of a story which would make her career, she did her researched between writing smaller articles on mundane local events which kept her boss happy. She called a contact at the Lottery office who informed her that personal information of winners could not be given out, however, she could be told which area the winning tickets were bought. One such winner was local, and the date was just before the killings started. She rang and told Harry who decided that if Andy was still their man, this would give him the means to buy the weapons. Added to the fact he suddenly moved house to a more expensive one, which meant a picture was forming, but they had no hard evidence, a good defense lawyer would call it circumstantial.

***

Andy was at home, drinking heavily, even though Jimbo waived him of any guilt, he still felt it. His mind was in over-drive and his soul crushed all because Jumbo's death couldn't be laid at any other door, but his own. It was another death on top of his wife, and children, that he felt responsible for. As a soldier responsibility for people's lives was an everyday accordance, which had now worn down his soul. If he hadn't told Jimbo of his quest, he would still have been alive, even if only for a few weeks, months or years more. In a bizarre way he envied him, because he believed that he was with all their old friends, just like Andy would love to be with his family once more. He put the TV on and on the News was an article about the fund raiser that Butterworth had been at. It was for a local orphanage; contact details were put on the screen and Andy wrote it down. He then wrote out a cheque for £40,000 for the cause and added a note simply saying, 'with regards Jimbo', and posted it that evening, while walking to the local pub. He thought Jimbo would appreciate it, as he had been raised in one, and had no immediate family. The pub was noisy, as it was darts night, the landlord asked him,

"Yes sir, what would you like?"

"Pint of Best please." Replied Andy.

"Nice to see you again, not seen you since the first time since you moved here. Dare say you have had much to do, took my wife and I, five years to get this place the way we wanted it."

"I don't have a wife." He was unable to say the word widow, as it would have clogged his throat like a ball-cock.

"Even more work for you then."

Andy paid and retired to a corner table, then watched all those around him enjoying themselves. The pain in his chest wouldn't go away, it wasn't illness, it wasn't indigestion, was it a thought of losing? He didn't know but maybe the answer was at the bottom of his glass, all he could see was another empty glass. After the second pint the memories came flooding back of happier times, with both families, the army and his most special family, as though they had come to visit his table in the corner of the bar to entertain him. His wife with both children playing surrounded by his comrades joking and reminiscing anecdotes of his youth. But after an hour or so they faded away, and were replaced by the landlord ringing the bell and calling time. As Andy was leaving the landlord called out,

"Goodnight Sir, everything alright? You seemed quiet tonight!"

"I'm sorry didn't mean to be rude or unsocial. It's my wedding anniversary today."

"Didn't your wife want to come out with you?"

"She would have loved it. She was ... always ... full of life. Goodnight!"

The landlord had seen that look before of a painful loss and said no more.

The following day Andy remembered Jimbo's dog (Duke) and decided to go and get him. Using his old clapped out car, the number plate was so dirty, no one could read it, but for now he saw that as an advantage. The dog Duke had been inside Jimbo's house all night and must need walking. On arrival at Jimbo's house, Police were about to enter, so Andy sat in his car across the road. Police had been called due to the neighbours hearing the dog barking all night followed by a deathly howl. The Police fearing there was a dead body inside forced the door and gained access. Duke, raced outside barking at them. In all the confusion Andy whistled and shouted "Duke", the dog raced towards him, he opened the door and the dog jumped inside then Andy drove off. There was not enough time for the Police to get the number plate, but they took note of the make and model. The two detectives didn't get a good look at the driver but were sure this could possibly be a partner in crime of Jimbo's. Mr. A!

Harry and Roger went back to the list supplied by Marion of possible suspects, even though Andy was at the top of the list as far as Harry was concerned, a second look was now in order. So, Marion called him,

"Harry, I've had an idea. What if I can get into see our Mr. Andy posing as a Solar Panel Representative, you see, many years ago while waiting for a Reporters job to be come available, I worked as one. I still have some calling cards and brochures that I could use, if I get in, I could possibly find out more about him!"

"As much as I appreciate you committing deception, and evidence gathered by entrapment ... I think! We could not use anything you find, as everything needs to be done by the book."

"I understand that Harry, but what if I find out his next target. He could leave papers lying around in his living room for all we know. He won't know who I am, and will not be concerned about leaving things in full view."

"OK, but please be careful."

***

A few hours later at Andy's house, he hid the car which may have been seen by the Police in an old barn of the property and covered it with an old canvas cover. About thirty minutes later Marion pressed the button of the security system,

"Hello." answered Andy

91

"Hello sir, my name is Marion and we are approaching all houses along this road. We are in the area fitting solar panels which would save you tons of money, and you don't pay anything. It's a Government incentive could I have just a moment of your time to show you in more detail."

Yet again the pretty face worked, the gates to the house opened and Marion drove in. Andy opened the front door, she was standing there dressed in a grey tight-fitting trouser suit.

"Come in Marion. I'm Andy."

On first impression, he did not seem a murderer, she even thought he was ruggedly handsome, with salt and pepper short hair. He took her through to the living room. She followed, admiring his athletic, yet mature build. She noticed a desk at the far end covered in papers, the walls were covered with photographs, painting a clear picture of his past. They sat, and Marion started the sales pitch that she used to roll off years ago. After about ten minutes he asked if she would like a cup of tea,

"Yes please, I'm parched."

"I won't be a minute then."

When he left the room, she got up and moved to the desk, pretending to look at a picture on the wall. She noticed a computer printout of a politician on the desk top and a newspaper opened to an article of one of the killings. Through the gap in the door and a carefully placed mirror, her every move was being watched by Andy. He smiled at her obvious amateur attempt to scan his home but, put it down to just being nosey. He thought to himself that she had reporter written all over her, but why come to him? He was intrigued and returned to the room sooner than she expected,

"Here we go, the kettle had only just boiled." He looked suspicious as she was close to his desk and she quickly said,

"Just admiring this picture."

"Just a print." He replied.

"William Blake isn't it."

"Yes, it is, great painter and poet." confirmed Andy.

"I see you were in the Army, going by those framed photographs?"

He didn't answer, just smiled.

They returned to their seats and carried on. As much as she tried, Andy would not divulge anything about himself through small talk.

"Well look it's been nice to talk to you Marion, but I have things to do. If you leave me your card, I will call you back when I've given it some thought. The roofs here are quite old and will need to be assessed before adding weight to it."

"I quite understand."

***

After leaving she went straight to see Harry,

"Harry, it worked … sort of! Didn't get any information out of him, but on his desk, was a print out of the politician Colin Black. Now he is well known for being involved in a pedophile scandal some years ago. Although never proven, there were other scandals of having links to organised crime. He's been in more cabinet reshuffles than a pack of cards."

"So, you think he could be next?"

"May be!" then she paused,

`   "There's something else. He seems really quite nice!"

"So now you think he's not our man? Well, I can assure you many seem nice. Ted Bundy came across intelligent and nice, but he was the opposite, quite the opposite! He murdered over thirty people!" she replied.

"OK! I get your point."

Chapter 10

A ndy sat at his desk with his laptop researching more on Colin Black, old damning articles and reports on this man were numerous, to the point Andy wondered how on earth he kept his position. A position Andy saw as one of trust, as his constituency trusted him to do what was best for them and the country. However, he was good in front of the camera and an audience. But the other side of his persona was very different.

In the next four days Andy followed at a distance, armed with a dictaphone and binoculars. On the fourth day, at 6pm, he followed him to an apartment block where he went inside carrying a carrier bag, containing three bottles of alcohol. Andy found a quiet corner spot of the car-park, where he got out his drone, with attached camera, from the boot of the car. He gave Black twenty minutes to get to which ever apartment had the party. It was a small exclusive building, consisting of twelve apartments within the three-story building. He flew the drone at a distance from each window and with the zoom could establish which window belonged to the party. As he moved along, one window on the end on the top floor was open with music blearing out. As it was now 6.30pm, the sun was low in the sky casting perfect light through the window which gave Andy a clear view of the inside, and of Black pouring large whiskeys. The bright light also absorbed the black coloured drone as it hovered in front of the sun as it filmed the scene. Black produced a small package from his coat pocket, which was hanging over a chair. The small party of twelve watched as he cut open the small packet on the glass top table. It contained a white powder which he started to make into lines the length of his credit card. After everyone had sniffed two lines each and downed several drinks, Black started to get extremely personal with a female guest who was dressed in the tightest of leather skirts. It was then obvious to Andy, that all the female guests were "Working Girls", the high-class type. Going by the body language of all, they were not strangers, which gave the impression this was a regular event.

Andy brought the drone back, after having seen enough. An idea started to manifest in his mind, that he could possibly use the film footage as leverage to make Black deliver a speech in Parliament, or else face a very public ruin. He was in two minds about whether Black was evil enough to execute, maybe he should be given a second chance to change. This on top of his already tarnished record would finish him.

***

The following morning Black, half asleep picked up his post. There was an A5 size Jiffy bag. Inside which he found a DVD and two envelopes.

One had 'Open this one first'. The other 'Open second'.

The first letter told him that the second letter was a speech for him to read out to the full house in Parliament. If he did not, then the DVD would be distributed to all the various media. Black made a strong coffee, and felt sick as he realised the letter was signed Mr. A, a name that had flown around government circles, they had hoped it would die a death and fade away like a bad dream. They all thought it was a short-lived thing and that he would, hopefully be caught by the Police. However, he was at large, and the letter was very direct, and to the point. Black had a spoilt upbringing, he became a party animal who threw his toys out if he didn't get his own way. There was an unsavory saying 'time to man up, and face responsibility.' His time had come. The medicine was not bitter sweet, but sour and smelled foul, it would cling to him for life. But at least there was hope, unlike the public release of the video which would send him to the pits of hell.

The day came when the House in Parliament was full, and it was Blacks turn to speak. Meanwhile the £40,000 cheque had arrived at the charity office which had caused quite a stir with such a generous donation. This only ever happened in the movies, and its news soon buzzed around.

Back in Parliament, Black had never been renowned for making a good speech, or even picking a good subject. He was a boring drunk who could organise great parties for many important people, many of whom were present and who also were customers for his drugs and prostitutes. It was this that he used as leverage to keep his own position. Many were surprised at his composed manner. Sober, and frightened, he started to sweat as he pulled out the speech, and cleared his throat,

"I have here a letter I would like to read to you, it reads, I am only alive because Mr. A want's this read out to you all.

As you are very much aware now, my mission is to cleanse our corrupt political, and judicial systems, both of which are paid for by the tax payer. The tax payer is your employer, yet while you live a life of luxury, the working person struggles. Those guilty of heinous crimes are let off lightly in the eyes of innocent. You send armed forces to fight illegal wars while you stay safe in your offices. The soldier can be found guilty of doing his duty, while you sip Earl Grey tea. Lawyers use the system and frequently lie to set scum free. Some Judges slap the wrists of scum that abuse young children, which begs the question why? Are they into that sick behavior too!"

He paused and looked around at all the faces in horror, but no one uttered a word. He carried on,

"The country has given millions, upon millions of pounds away to various countries in aid over many, many years and yet these countries do not improve because much of the money is filtered off by rich politicians, and organized crime syndicates. I want what the public want, an end to all of this. You may say that this cannot be done overnight, and I understand that, but people work harder and faster when there is an incentive, so I will give you that incentive.

You have one week to make some fundamental changes to prove you are taking this seriously. Sacking crooked Politicians and Judges takes no time at all and I dare say you can speed up other issues too, it's up to you. Just keep in mind the incentive, which is, if I am not satisfied on the eighth day, then every other day . . . you will all lose a colleague . . . who's history is full of corruption. The ones of you who are straight as a dye, need not worry. Those who are not, best change your ways very publicly, or become the next possible target. I am going to judge scum, and they will answer to me, if my demands are not met. For now, I am Judge, Jury and Executioner. I am Mr. A"

The house at first went quiet, then errupted into accusations, and character assassinations, which were thrown back and forth. Front Bench and Back Bench alike, were all throwing abuse into the heated air. Black sank onto his seat, trembling for he knew Mr. A. had so much knowledge about , and he could be next. Maybe, the part regarding changing one's ways publicly was aimed at him. If he confessed publicly to drug addiction, and put himself into rehab, plus pass the details of his drug contacts to the Police, he just may save himself. The drugs people would not be happy, but he could get himself body guard, and write it off against expenses. His mind was a buzz, as indeed so was every other head in the house. A complete media blackout was implemented. However, it did not last long as too many people were present and saw the opportunity to discredit the opposition.

The next morning, it was on You Tube, Facebook and Twitter, all with burning hot fingers on keyboards were expressing their views. Within the next few days the media was full of the news that many Judges had been fired, along with many Politicians. The days of discredited people being demoted had gone. The threat by Mr. A was real, so there could be no half measures. The aid issue also made the news, in respect it was being cut by 50%. Cuts came from those countries that truly did not require it. It was then moved to improve conditions for land troops. The Government could act on most requests made by Mr. A. but, crooked lawyers were not something they could do anything about, however, there was movement in their circles and rumours, that some companies were letting go those who performed below the level of excellence. Any who had a questionable history, were shown the door, with the excuse, "Sorry but you are a liability".

The news of the £40,000 cheque for the charity found its way to Harry, also the fact that the name Jimbo was used,

"According to the name on the cheque, it's from Mr. A. McIntosh. A lot of money. Why? But it also proves nothing."

"Maybe payment in memory of someone called Jimbo!" replied Rog.

"Maybe our burnt-up corpse that was found in the Land Rover! But giving money to charity is hardly evidence."

"Can we prove the body was this Jimbo?"

"There's not even dental, the explosion saw to that." replied Harry.

"He really has the Government by the balls!" said Roger as he gulped his coffee.

***

Harry tossed and turned in bed that night, as did Andy while the stories on the internet started to multiply, and go viral. By the morning, most of Europe, and America, had heard about the infamous Mr. A. holding the British Government to ransom. One headline read, 'Once an Empire, demolished by one man'. Opinion polls were balanced, those in favour of the clear out of corruption, and those who hated the rest of the world for laughing at their once proud country.

***

It was day six, and even though movement had been made, Andy was not yet satisfied. Although he knew he had asked much, and Rome wasn't built in a day, he was impatient to see a sign. With each day that passed he felt the Police breathing down his neck, the only thing that kept them at bay was lack of evidence, much to the annoyance of Detective Inspector Harry Harper, who's gut feeling was starting to feel like an ulcer ready to burst. He and Detective Sergeant Roger Williams still tried to keep an eye on him, and his movements, but Andy was too clever. He was reading the local paper, "The Echo" and an article about a local young soldier sent back home, from active duty, minus his legs, left arm and left eye. Before being shipped out to do his duty, he had got married, and while abroad given the news that he was to be a Father. Andy could appreciate the feelings which ran through the young man's veins, however, it was the headline that caught Andy's eye,

'Young soldier to lose home!'

He could not afford the high rents that now were the norm for a small house. Andy grabbed his cheque book and made his way to the Echo's office. By sheer luck it was Marion who saw him and asked if she could help. He explained he wanted to help the couple, and needed to know how to find them.

"So, if you have directions? By the way! Not in Solar Panels anymore?" he asked.

"No. I got bored." She replied.

" …and found a new job in less than a week, Wow! Fast mover!" he smiled.

It was not the done thing, but Marion offered to take him,

"Leave your car here and I'll take you, saves you struggling to find it." She suggested.

"Your kind, thanks! You would think the Government would help people in such a position." Andy replied.

"Well Yes! …but it's the system lack of funds." she laughed, "and yet so much money is wasted elsewhere. I wrote an article about a small industrial estate on the outskirts of town using Government funds so to attract new business to the town …cost millions!" replied Marion.

"That's not wasting money to bring work in?" questioned Andy.

"It is when they stand empty for 8 years, one building is occasionally hired out for short periods. All because some idiot didn't do his research. The main route from here to the motorway is too far and congested, compared to the City, which virtually sits on the motorway ... logistics you see for transporting goods." She said, then continued with in depth knowledge. Andy was impressed!

"Our town once had a train station, but back in the 60's Dr. Richard Beeching closed many of the small stations because they were deemed not cost effective. If only that one had been re-thought. As now we have cluttered roads and just maybe ... it may have brought more business to our small town ... who knows!"

Andy looked at her and slowly smiled, then with a slightly sarcastic tone said,

"For someone selling solar panels one week, then a clerical worker in a news room the next. You really sound like a seasoned reporter with a good grasp of local history especially political history."

"Are you interested in political history, or politics?" she asked.

Andy did not reply, but turned away and stared out the car window to where a tramp was pushing a super market trolley, contained all his worldly possessions,

"See him!" he asked

"Yes." She replied.

"There's a story for you. It said inside everyone is a good book. Their life story, which to themselves may seem mundane, even boring. But to others, it's an adventure, a different way of life. I've known people with lots of money, but no life.

I have known Generals pat themselves on the back for a job well done, even though they were thousands of miles away from the action. I have known a squaddie use his body to shield his team from grenade, giving his life to save others in a selfless act. There are good and bad at all levels, and all with a story to tell."

"Are you trying to tell my something?" she asked.

"Old saying, do not judge a book by its cover. The smartest dressed man can hide the devil himself, yet a tramp could be God in disguise. If you're going to report on a subject, strip away the layers of Christmas wrapping paper to reveal the gift, otherwise you may end up with a booby prize." He profoundly remarked.

"Are you saying all those in authority are selfish bigots." she asked.

"No! Of course not. But a rotten apple can spoil the whole crop, unless it is removed. Did you know, that if you leave a rotten apple next to good ones, then the mold spores spread, infecting the nice apples. Removing the rotten apple is like removing a cancer growth, you get it in time before it spreads." He described.

"You see yourself as a surgeon? Would you like to remove them" she asked? Making him laugh, as her probing was becoming uncomfortable, and too close for comfort, so he didn't reply.

***

They arrived at the young soldier's tiny modern built house and were invited inside. Andy pulled out his cheque book and sat in a chair, while the soldier's wife made tea in the kitchen with Marion helped and chatted.

"I read in the paper about you and your wife having to leave your home." Andy asked.

"Yes, embarrassing. But we wanted people to know what happens. Don't get me wrong the Army have been great. Got me some new artificial legs and arm, but they can't help with a career ... earning money! I didn't expect to end up this way, and all because the fucking vehicle we were in didn't have proper armoured plating ... no better than a standard Landy or a Baked Bean tin. The mine ripped through it and I was the lucky one! My mate, he ... he." The words could not leave his mouth as he croaked an apology. Andy then tried to relate to his story,

"I was blown up once, but it was an open top Landy and I was blown clear."

"You're a Veteran then?"

"Yes ... but enough about our pasts, let's look to the future. What would you like to do?"

I still have my right arm; hand and I'm right handed ... so there's a blessing. In time with more training they reckon I'll be able to drive an adapted car, which I can't afford. Working in a warehouse maybe or something like that, but 8 hours later my stumps would hurt. I guess if I did half that and half sat on my ass earning money would be good. I used to write short stories before the Army ... one got published too in a magazine. I could try that again."

"Really! Well in that case if someday I give you a rough draft and notes with pictures, you could do my autobiography."

"Are you famous then, as publishers are only interested in famous people or writers that had already published good sellers."

"Famous! Not yet!" replied Andy

"What regiment were you in?"

"Teas up!" his wife called out as she and Marion re-appeared from the kitchen.

"So, what have you men been talking about?" she asked.

"Andy was in the Army too." replied the soldier

"Long time ago … and old news, let's look to the future. I had a little luck a while ago and came into money, which I would like to share with you." Announced Andy.

The young soldier looked shocked, then his pride took over,

"Andy that's very kind, but I've always worked to support myself and family. Charity is all well and good for those that really need it but … " this made Andy laugh! and he pointed at the missing legs,

"Missing both legs, an arm and an eye! and you say you don't need it!"

The very black humour made both of them laugh while the ladies looked on in amazement as the young soldier replied,

"As in the famous words of the Python Black Knight … It's only a scratch!" again made both roared with laughter, bringing a smile to the ladies faces and a tear in his wife's eye. This was the first time since he had come out of hospital, that he had had a laugh!

Andy pulled out a pen and wrote a cheque, the soldier then told Andy,

"Look its very kind of you, but we will sort this out, the paper gave us a small cheque for the story which helped pay off one month's rent arrears."

"This is not charity, this is payment for my soul. I served many years, in many situations all over the world and came out in one piece. It seems to me you got my share of bad luck and received injuries for two or three men. You sir are a hero, and we must look after our heroes." And he handed him the cheque.

The young man shook uncontrollably and passed the cheque to his wife, she brought her hand to her mouth in shock,

"But this is too much!"

"There is a proviso on this money too. When I've finished the draft, I want you to write the book of my exploits and publish it along with photos of my military years. I am sure you will have no trouble finding a publisher."

Andy knew that what he said was true but couldn't elaborate on the fact for obvious reasons. The soldier's wife showed the cheque to Marion, who's eyes bulged at the sight of the £200,000 cheque.

"It's enough for the work you will have to do, it will buy you a modest house and have some left over to tie you over until your lives are back on track."

The young man shook his hand with both hands, tears weld up in his eyes as his wife threw her arms around Andy as a thank you. Marion with mixed emotions was confused to see the suspect in so many murders be so compassionate. She didn't know whether to laugh, cry, hate him or love him. She was sure of one thing, there was more to this story than meets the eye, and something she would have to relay to Detective Inspector Harper.

***

Later that day in Harry's office, she relayed on what she knew. Harry was amazed at Marion's story, which left him feeling perplexed,

"A suspect with a heart . . . well that's a first!" then noticed that Marion knew more,

"There's more, what is it?" asked Harry.

"The whole Mr. A. story has got our editor thinking, because he's hit only crooked people that we portrayed in many of our past articles, he sees him more as a Robin Hood, then a Jack the Ripper. If it wasn't for political correctness and Government pressure, he would publish very different story, and if he knew what we now know, he would! For so many years a corrupt world has hidden behind Corporate and Government curtains, that shine bright, to blind us of what lies behind them." She exclaimed as though delivering a speech on the world stage.

"That was very eloquently put. But it is not for us to judge, that is for a Judge to do." Which made Detective Sergeant Roger Williams smile,

"That's right, just like the crooked ones that got pushed out the other day. Sorry Harry, but I do see her point, and his, to a degree! It's getting to the point that I don't know who the crooks anymore."

"I'll pretend I didn't hear that. We are Police officers, here to uphold the law. Plain and simple! Even if it's all screwed up." Replied Harry in a serious tone, to which Rog replied,

"From a boy I wanted to be a Policeman, I would read a comic book, which the crook carried a bag with SWAG written on it and wore a mask. Now they carry a laptop and wear a suit. Even judges wear a suits and carry laptops, the crook has no mask anymore, they hide in plain sight behind passwords, and binary codes, and of course the grey areas of the law."

Harry laughed, "Yes, it's a mad world"

Chapter 11

On day seven of Mr. A's ultimatum, the national news covered the story of the national cleanup of the judicial system. 15 judges were discredited and given early retirement, 90 senior police officers were given the same treatment. 30 politicians were sacked, and overseas aid was halved followed by a section on private law firms who cleaned up their act with sackings and early retirements. Andy was pleased and yet he asked himself would they keep it up. Was the information true and what of the Armed Forces and illegal wars, there was nothing on that at all. So, he sent another add to the paper by post with a simple request. It found its way into the next days paper, was read by those in power,

"So far, so good, but what of the Soldiers of this once proud land.

O Death where is your Glory,

O Death, where is your Sting.

Those on the frontline found it in the lack of support and armour. Was this not an area to be reviewed? If it was not, and no movement not seen by tomorrow, then another, relative to that subject, will also feel my sting.

There is no place to hide."

***

Panic ran through the Houses of Parliament and offices of those who dealt with such matters. Andy already had a target marked out, a middle-aged MP called Hyde. Even though he had left a clue, it fell on deaf ears. Hyde was a man who had been moved from pillar to post over the years. When there were cabinet reshuffles, he was often in them. Not really thinking about his work, or responsibilities, he was more interested in his good friend, Mr. Black's parties. It's a small world, Andy thought. Hyde also had dealings in Companies that were less than honest, even though he sat on the board of Directors he ignored the illegal conduct it was involved with regards selling arms to dishonest countries, who were constantly at war with their neighbours. Hyde ignored the request by the Police to change his daily routine, making Andy's job easier, except Hyde lived in an apartment in London.

He planned to eliminate Hyde by means of a long-range sniper shot from a tall building. As irony would have it, Mr. Hyde, every Wednesday afternoon, would take a packed lunch to Hyde Park and sit on the same bench opposite the lake. He would sit and imagine the park was named after him, he was that vain. At first, he thought he was a bird lover watching the ducks, however, it was a different type of bird that caught his eye. One that jogged through the park at the same day and time each day. She was young enough to be his daughter, Andy thought. She was blonde, slim, a very fit student. Andy guessed she was a student by her youthful look, she wore a sweatshirt of a local University. He took position on a roof top, and watched through his scope, the rifle barrel rested on a small bean bag. Hyde tucking into a sandwich as the girl jogged by, he smiled and said,

"Afternoon pretty lady." She half smiled and quickened her pace.

Hyde's head was in the cross hairs of Andy's scope as his finger covered the trigger. Then his view became blocked as a woman stopped with her pram and picked up a crying baby to comfort it. Hyde's face turned showed annoyance as the crying baby was spoiled his lunch. He took a swig from a water bottle that was the colour of cold tea, possibly whiskey. Andy started to wish the woman would move but she stood there rocking the baby who became quiet once more. Hyde's face showed enjoyment, as another young female jogger came into view. The woman put the baby slowly back into the pram and smiled. Hyde finished his last sandwich as she left, leaving Andy clear shot, Hyde stood up ready to leave, then paused as the jogger went by,

"Afternoon pretty lady." she too upped her paced.

Andy placed his finger on the trigger as Hyde tossed his small bag of rubbish at a near by bin. It missed and fell to the ground, but he didn't care and turned to walk away exposing his temple. Andy held his breath and focused as he squeezed the trigger. Seconds later Hyde's brains decorated the bench in an abstract fashion, his knees buckled, and he collapsed to the floor.

Andy calmly dismantled the rifle and put it with the bean bag into a rucksack and made his way back to his newly bought motorbike, which had false plates, he rode off, taking back routes wherever possible. There was no need for the signature papers anymore, his action was well known and feared.

To add interest, and tease for Harry, he left a note topped with the empty bullet casing, minus the fingerprints

***

Back home he changed the plates and hid the false ones in a bag in his compost heap. He made a sandwich and watched the evening news which reported his latest killing. So did the amateur reports on the internet but was more graphic and honest with the truth.

He went to the local pub where he got chatting to a retired man who had been in for there a while, so his tongue was more loose than normal and he proceeded to tell him his life story, until he divulged that he once worked for British Intelligence,

" ... of course, we were sworn to the official secrets act, but these days at my time of life I think, what the hell. We once had a marvelous country, but it's gone downhill since the good old days"

"Meaning?" asked Andy.

"Well ... I can tell you, but mind you, between you me and the gate post, what's happening abroad worry's me ... I still have my contacts and it's obvious that certain groups of people are being fed false information, bringing them here, stating that life here is a dream. The Government will give you a house, a car and money to live a life of luxury without working for it." the man said

"Surely not! Everyone knows that you don't get something for nothing." replied Andy.

"That is true, however young man, I can assure you the world today is very different than the one when we were young. These days you can have Charities as fronts for terrorist groups, raising cash for recruits. Super rich families dictating to Banks and Governments. Forces are at work to cripple the

West and I don't mean the Russians, that was much easier." and he laughed! Then continued,

"Ah! Yes, the good old days, we knew the enemy quite well too at times, first name terms and all that. Now he's faceless, a number, a machine, an idea, or a damn religion."

Andy felt sorry for the old man who went on to tell him more,

"I went to Sandhurst, following in a bit of a family tradition. After the war I left the Army and entered the Civil Service, then MI6, it was then I realised how dirty life could be ... but now it's worse. I can safely say that Intelligence is even more important now, than ever before. Good intelligence saves lives, I think I need a refill of Scotch and water, would you like another?"

"That's kind, but no. I must go shortly, have paperwork to catch up on." replied Andy, he thought about the book of himself for the young soldier.

They chatted for a little longer and all the man talked about fueled Andy's thirst for his quest. He felt bad having to leave the old chap who enjoyed off-loading his whole life story, but Andy decided that his one pint was enough, he wanted to get started on the notes for the book he promised, so he shook hands and wished him well, then left for home.

He showered and sat at his desk and typed out the notes in date order of his life. The military aspects were open and honest and held nothing back. After six long hours of typing he collected pictures together and put them into a folder, then he poured a large Whiskey, slumped into his chair and stared at a picture of his family in better times, then he slowly fell into a deep sleep.

***

The following morning the main news item was of Hyde, but this time more detail was aired. The shot was so clean and accurate, the finger was pointed at Mr. A. In the Prime Minister's office, it was argued that not enough had been done regarding the Military, it had been overlooked and forgotten,

"Well he didn't forget." shouted the PM.

"We know Sir, but we need more time to execute changes."

"Oh! I see! So, in the meantime this Mr. A can execute one of us at a time. Stop fucking about, make it happen and advertise the fact. I want to see top brass singing our praises on TV. In the meantime, catch this fucking madman, before he takes a pop shot at me!"

"But where do we get the funding Sir?"

The PM picked up the phone,

"Good morning! Prime minister here, give me George...Hello George! That £80 million you wanted to invest in in that project overseas. ...Yes, that's the one, sorry but you've lost it. It's going to pay for armour and support for the Army...I know it puts you in an awkward position, but let me put this to you George, it's that or a certain Mr. A. will find out where the money went and might get a little miffed! Yes George. I kid you not. Bye George, regards to your family."

The room stood in silence seeing that the Prime Minister was going to move to great lengths to appease Mr. A. He carried on with a determined demeanor.

"There you have £80 million, and it's 9.15am you have 24 hours to move heaven and earth to make Top Brass sing our praises, or your fired too! Meantime I will find another £40 million to add to that, it's going to piss off a few people."

Meanwhile Andy decided that a direct letter to the Prime Minister was in order and so took a break from the book notes.

Inspector Harper and Sergeant Williams were having a heated discussion,

"Look Rog. I thought I would ask for 24 hr. surveillance on our Mr. Andy, so how did he get out to commit this hit on Hyde?"

"Yes, but the constable was called out to an RTI (Road Traffic Incident), he couldn't have been gone more than 30 minutes!"

"Long enough for him to leave but should have seen him come back?" pointed out Harry.

"Well yes but ... " replied Roger.

"But what?" asked Harry.

"There was a delay in the switch over by all accounts so there could have been no one there between 7 and 8 that evening." Winced Roger.

"Bloody Hell! We must do better than this. From now on I want someone there 24/7, no excuses!"

"Yes Sir."

"Brief the men. If it happens again, heads will roll."

Andy was aware of the surveillance and had planned a way out from his property via the bottom of the garden, using his dirt motorbike. He could use the farmers access routes across the fields, this would take him to a back lane, then onto the main road. He set up timers on all the house lamps, to give the impression that he was at home.

***

Later that day he walked to the local post box, with Duke, to post the Prime Ministers letter. He noticed a man whom he assumed to be a Policeman in plain clothes, sitting in a car reading a paper, which he thought was a big give away. It gave him the idea that he would not use the post again, they just might check the post box contents next time. That night the evening news had an article about the sudden investment by the Government, for protection, and support, for the armed forces. Much to Andy's pleasure and surprise at the Top Brass. For the first time in history the powers that be, really did make things happen quickly, just how it must be in the business world, much to the shock of the rest of the cabinet, and media.

In the morning, the rain hammered down in Downing Street. Gossip flew around about threats given, and promises made, to raise the needed money, by slashing none important budgets. Many politicians woke with monumental headaches, and hangovers from the night before, after drowning their sorrows. The PM's private secretary brought in the morning post. Andy's type written letter was on top. He opened it and started to read,

***

'Let me start by saying I am pleased that you have taken me seriously, however, there is still much required for me to cease my actions. You cannot deny that corruption floods the corridors of power, unless this is something you condone. A corrupt British government is no better than the ones our armed forces are sent out to fight. A world leader must do just that, lead by example. The media is full of stories about corruption at Whitehall, right through to the local councils. Can you sit there and say this is all media hype? No, I think not! Do you want to go down in history as just another Prime Minister who did a job, or the Prime Minister who changed the face of Britain? Maybe the man that people will put on a shelf equal to Churchill? Do you have the vision and the guts to attempt this, are you like the others, who just see the position to gain wealth? Search your conscience, delve into your very soul to find the obvious answer or, should I assume you will treat this letter with contempt. I hope you will see and listen to the people who have had enough of bad Government. I look forward to your reply in the private ads of the Echo newspaper.

Yours sincerely

Mr. A.'

***

The PM gave the letter to his private secretary then got up from his desk and went to the window. The secretary started to read whilst the PM was deep in thought, looking out at a cloudy day, part of him saying the guy is a nut, with another part saying there was too much truth in what he said. Was this a mad dream? Could it be done? He could not deny that the gamble was appealing, however, it could also be political suicide. Maybe he might be killed by the secret service, who in turn would blame Mr. A. He swallowed heavily as his stomach churned over.

The secretary finished reading the letter and he placed it back on the desk,

"It's well written, but there are no specific demands."

The PM did not reply, he just stood motionless as though at that moment nothing else mattered. He watched the heavy rain lash the window, on the pavement below the gutters were full of rushing rain water, washing any muck that lay there down the sewer, cleansing the streets of unwanted dirt. Was this what Mr. A. was doing? In turn offering the prime minister the chance to cleanse the corridors of power. The secretary gave an awkward cough,

"Prime Minister? Do you want to reply to it?"

"How long have we known each other John?" he replied.

The secretary, John, was not used to being addressed by his first name, in fact it was the first time the PM had done it,

"10 years this July, Sir."

"What I say to you never leaves this office does it?" quizzed the Prime Minister.

"No Sir...never!" which was true.

"Do you think it could be done?" the PM asked.

"What Sir...clean up politics in general. You know me Sir, I have always tried to do my job to the best of my ability, serve you and indirectly serve the country. My father served in the army during the last war, I wanted to follow, but failed the physical, this was the next best way I could serve." John replied.

"Your leading up to what John?"

"I believe in the justice system. I believe in truth, honesty, integrity and I am afraid many within the walls of Parliament do not. There are those that play the system, and use it for their own means. You have dismissed and moved a sizable number of these people, but there are many more. The problem is Sir, a few of those are good at their job. Siphoning through the trash, so to speak, will take a long time."

Both stood in silence then John added,

"If you intend on bending to this man's will then..."

"What? I'm a fool, an idiot...let's face it we've cowed to terrorism in the past why should this be different?" The PM asked.

"Because Sir, this is different! You go ahead with this then you are a bigger..."

"Wanker!" the PM laughed.

"No! A bigger man than I thought. You do this and get it right; the people will love you for it. You will make enemies along the way, and people will try to destroy you. However, I believe social media now steer's the worlds press and will back you, as I would." John sincerely replied.

"Good as I can't do this on my own. I don't trust everyone else not to let this out to the press. After all, I don't want the rats leaving the ship before I've stamped on them." Quipped the PM.

"Quite Sir, but this ship will not sink! After all, Britannia rules the waves!"

Chapter 12

Andy was researching the next target, although he hoped his letter had some effect, which it had. The PM asked his secretary to request the attendance of the Detective working on the case,

"I understand that it is Detective Inspector Harper." said John.

"Ask him to come to London and see me." said the PM.

"Don't you mean his superior?"

"No, get me Harper."

"You could just phone Sir." John pointed out.

"Yes, but we both know these calls have been intercepted before." Came the reply.

It was quite a shock to Harry Harper to be asked to number ten. He received the call at 10am and was standing at the door by 2.30pm. He exchanged pleasantries with the constable on the door and was shown in. He was not kept waiting and was ushered into see the PM who greeted him,

"Detective Inspector Harry Harper do sit down. I understand you oversee the Mr. A' case."

"That is correct Prime Minster."

"I want to speak freely and frankly, completely off the record ... don't worry there are no bugs in here, that is why I asked you to come in person and not chat on the phone."

"I'm sorry Prime Minister, who would want to listen apart from Mr. A. and the press."

"Plenty! You see, as much as it pains me to admit, Mr. A. is quite right. There were, and still are, rotten apples in the basket. As per his demands I moved many on, but there are still some remaining. It is those who remain that are a problem. People with overseas connections have such influence, that if I was to sever their political career, sanctions would be brought into affect against our country. It's all very messy!" pointed out the PM.

"I understand that to a degree Prime Minister, but what do you want of me? I am trying to catch Mr. A. with bullet proof evidence, so he will go down for good. Yet we have not been able get enough rock-solid evidence. He is extremely clever, resourceful, and a well-trained individual. I have no evidence but, I believe him to possibly be ex special forces such as ... " the PM raised his hand.

"Don't mention his name please! As at this point, he is a suspect that is all, with no evidence. You see Harry ... may I call you Harry?"

"Please do!" feeling extremely honoured.

"At this moment, he has hit out at those within the political community, who ... shall we say, are less than honest. One could say crooks dressed up as politicians. However, there are also some slightly tarnished individuals who are extremely good at their job...I hope Mr. A. can tell the difference. So far, he has, thank God."

"Sorry Prime Minister, but it almost sounds as though you agree, or support him."

"Do you Inspector? How many times have you wanted to put a pedophile or a crooked politician behind bars, but they were untouchable?"

Harry could not answer, even though he wanted to shout YES! The PM continued,

"Your silence speaks volumes Inspector. As I said at the beginning, what is said here is between you and I. No one else, not even your most trusted friends and loved ones can know of what we say."

"Yes Sir."

"Are you a gambling man?" asked the Prime Minister

"The odd flutter on the lottery!" smiled Harry.

"I mean gamble on knowing your gut instinct to be right."

"I get a gut feeling occasionally."

"Like with Mr. A...well Inspector, I am going to gamble that this man could, for the moment, help me clean up the Government and Judicial system. In other words, I would appreciate you not working so hard to catch him but being seen to be doing your job. You could make sure his identity is kept as a low profile, as though he is at the bottom of your list, as I assume you have mentioned to colleagues you suspect him?" The PM ordered.

"That's a tall order sir!"

"I do realise that, but it will come with benefits and appreciation in due course, such as promotion, with increased pension rights."

"Isn't this bordering on what Mr. A. is fighting against, bribes?"

"Not at all. This is a small benefit that affects only you. He is against the multimillion affairs which affect every taxpayer and the security of this this country."

"I suppose so Sir, but"

"I am like you Harry. I came from a working-class background, which I kept hidden very well. My father worked his fingers to the bone, so I could go to the best University. It changed my life, but there are times when I wish I was working in a foundry like he did, away from the silver spooned crooks, that dictate to the masses. Don't get me wrong, there are more good ones than bad. Ones at the very top are decent people, but below the top ranks are political "wannabees", who fuel drugs, sex and greed. Like you I would like to see them whipped away. My father died of cancer not long after I became PM, the price he paid for years in the foundry. So, that I could become such a man. He hated crooked systems, he believed in a UK of old which doesn't exist anymore, because of a cancer that was growing within the Government, spurned by those greedy individuals. I owe it to him, to make his dream come true and I think maybe Mr. A. has started the ball rolling. The cancer now has an enemy, seeking them out, and I don't want him stopped ... not just yet!"

Harry was unsure how to feel, as he saw it, he was going to have to become a bent copper, to meet the PMs wishes and keep it secret from Roger.

***

The following day Andy read a cryptic advert placed in the paper by the PM which no one else was aware of, except his secretary John.

'Mr. A. Thanks for starting spring clean, will carry on clearing, and throwing out rubbish. Please refrain from too much cleaning, as sometimes you may throw out something valuable. Keep in touch. Regards PM'

Andy read it three times as it came as a surprise. To him it had almost friendly undertones. Could it be that he was being thanked and waved on to get rid of the true hardened scum who contaminated the corridors of power? This needed a strong coffee, and deep thought, as he paced up and down, walking from room to room. He looked out of the windows to where the plain clothes policeman would be sitting in a car...he wasn't there. He checked in all directions, but there was no one! He was either off their radar, or the PM had them called off. His newspaper advert was lenient to almost friendly, which gave Andy the impression, he was doing the PM a favour.

***

Meantime, Marion's file on the evidence and theory of the case was growing. Each day she set aside one hour, to write her story ready for when the case came to rest. Harry would then give her the go ahead to publish it in the papers.

Meanwhile Andy had sent a memory stick of his full story, plus photographs, to the young ex-soldier, who was writing his autobiography. This was being written with great enthusiasm and the use of the internet to find pictures of the more famous campaign that Andy had fought in. Detective Inspector Harry Harper, on the other hand was shouting the odds-on having Andy's house watched 24/7 and had called them away leaving him alone. He tried to explain his actions to Rog,

"Roger it's simple, we have no firm evidence on our Mr. Andy, so it doesn't warrant the overtime. It could also be seen as Police harassment."

Roger was in shock and replied,

"Well this is the first time I've seen you turn your back on a gut feeling!"

Harry knew that Roger would not let this lie,

"Ok, Ok! I had word from them above to cut back on unnecessary expenditure, the budget has been slashed and we have to comply, and adjust to the financial climate change, or some such crap!" He thought that actually sounded good and Roger swallowed it too!

Chapter 13

The Prime Minister with his secretary was organising letters to out to twenty individuals who they had managed to dig up dirt on or, good reasons for dismissing them from their Government positions. The reasons ranged from sexual harassment of female staff, fiddling expenses, fraudulent CV's and the giving or receiving bribes. The hard part was to replace them with good stock! This is when the secretary proved his worth because of his grasp of local gossip, and general knowledge of those within government circles. The Prime Minster never realised just how much he didn't know about his own staff, only John!

***

For the next three days, this was the daily routine and by Friday, a press release was sent out, under the title of "Cabinet Reshuffle". Andy was so pleased that he treated himself to a small bottle Scotch. Harry and Roger carried on as usual, except in the back of Harry's mind was the secret conversation with the PM, which weighed heavily on his mind, and his stomach ulcer. While in many houses that evening ex government employees were pulling their hair out, John was organising a flight for the PM. Known as a 'Good Will' visit to a Middle Eastern country which had seen years of trouble, but now things seemed to be coming together and had experienced a full two years of trouble-free time. The PM's schedule was to promote and seal trade deals, worth billions. Both sides gained, received investment, technical and engineering help, in return for advantageous trade deal.

That night Andy could see the light at the end of the tunnel. His plan was coming true, he sat and looked at the picture of his wife, children, and toasted them,

"I know you would have disagreed with the way I went about things, but the result was worth it ... God bless you." For once that night he had a peaceful, deep, sleep.

The following morning John wished the PM a successful trip,

"Good luck Prime Minister see you in a few days."

"Thank you, John, I know you have come on these trips with me before in the past. However, it's more important that you are my eyes and ears here after what I've been up to. There are many sore heads this morning I dare say, you know what to do, keep me informed."

Within an hour he was on his flight, and the first of the irate phone calls to John about the reshuffle started, but he was an expert at handling bad tempered ex-employees, whom he knew could afford to be out of work for a considerable time, and walk into other high-profile jobs within six months. As for Andy, he was still asleep in his armchair, with an empty Scotch bottle on the floor next to him. Harry and Roger were slowly following up rubbish leads from the Mr. A. case; which

Harry knew were a waste of time. But it meant they were well away from drawing attention to Andy.

***

On the plane the Prime Minister was relaxing on his flight, thinking about the drastic changes he had made in, and around the government cabinet, it left him feeling positive. He was also pleased that two other visits he was to make, after this one had been cancelled, as he didn't want to be away for too long. He was brought a cup of tea as he read the paper which was full of the news of the Government reshuffle. The articles were positive, with one saying that it was a brave move, and another saying the Prime Minister was,

'Throwing out the rotten apples to make way for new fruit, and a brighter future.'

That one put a beaming smile on his face, making him feel that if he had the press, and the people behind him. He could achieve anything. He gazed out the window, with the Mediterranean glistening blue as the plane approached the coastline of his destination.

***

Back home Andy read in the paper that the PM was away. He decided not to do anything until he returned. After all he was making things happen. So, he got on with some jobs around the house, and of course prepared kit and weapons . . . just in case.

Harry, hearing of the PM being out of the country decided to use the spare few days to clear up paperwork that had built up over the past months. His desk was starting to resemble a recycling centre on a bad day.

The next few days flew by for all of them, and the PM found himself flying back after an extremely successful visit and with deals signed, the future was looking brighter by the minute. For the first time in his term of office, he felt a sense of real achievement, all because of Mr. A's hard handed approach. Tea was served, and he caught up with the news by looking at the internet. In general, the comments, and articles about him and the reshuffle was getting great support, apart from some of those who had been on the receiving end, who found colourful language useful in expressing themselves. He sipped his tea and passed the tablet to his police bodyguard,

"Here have a browse and give me your honest opinion."

"Thank you, Sir. But it is not for me to have an opinion, to compliment, or criticize you Sir."

"Oh! Bollocks. We are all friends here, I'm a grown man, I can take it!"

The policeman grinned,

"I voted for the other guy I'm afraid, but now I am glad you won. Now, I see what you can do, maybe we will get the government which everyone has wanted, but never got."

"Well, thank you! That is my aim. God willing, I will achieve it."

BANG! A siren went off, air masks fell in front of them, also, the sensation of the plane diving. The pilot made a frantic SOS radio call as the plane drew ever closer to the sparkling Mediterranean Sea, which a short while ago seemed so pleasing but was now became threatening, a grave. The pilot's message, though weak, was received and RAF jets were scrambled, as well as an Air Sea Rescue crew from a nearby base. Outside, the scream of the plummeting plane could be heard inside, adding the fear to everyone, whose racing hearts and minds felt helplessly doomed. The PM sent a text to John, it was to be his last request. The policeman grabbed the PM's hand and said quivering,

"I am so sorry Sir, there's nothing I can do!"

"That's quite alright. I am sorry for you having to pay for my actions in Government."

The policeman smiled and winked,

"For the greater cause Prime Minister. It's been an honour Sir."

By the time the jets got to the position, there was nothing to be found. The plane had crashed into a watery grave.

***

Johns mobile notified him that he had received a text, he opened it, and instantly his heart shot into his throat as he read it,

"We are hit, last message, in safe brown envelope, DVD play it, read documents. Thanks John, you're a great friend. Goodbye, my honourable friend."

Then completely out of character he poured a Whiskey and downed it in one. He went to the safe and sat in the PM's chair and watched the DVD.

"Hello John. If you're watching this, then I am dead. I made this using my iPhone, a few days ago before I flew off on the Middle Eastern trip. The papers on that visit are on their way to you via a courier. You see John, MI6 warned me of a threat. I took all precautions apart from taking condoms . . . ha ha! You and I have achieved a lot, and now I am afraid it's down to you and my replacement. You will find all necessary files, and information in the brown envelope. Please pass the other on to my family. God bless you and be strong, because the wolves will be out now. However, you are more than capable. One more thing there is one piece of info in that file. You

MUST memorize it then destroy it; it is marked for your eyes only. Cheers John."

He opened the envelope, it contained papers for his replacement, a man John had always liked who was fair, honest, and as tough as old boots. A sort of old school type in his late 50's. Other papers related to the work they both worked on, with the next forms of action. He opens a small envelope marked 'your eyes only, read and destroy'.

It was brief information on Andy with contact details. He knew instantly that it was imperative he spoke to him, before the media heard the news.

***

As he drove to Andy's home, his mind was full of scenarios of the near future. Although John knew that this information was only known by both him and Detective Inspector Harry Harper, he was not going to take chances because he did not know why the plane had crashed, and whether it was deliberate. So soon after the reshuffle was too convenient.

It was just over three hours later that he drew near. He pulled over as it occurred to him that maybe having Harry there too would be a promising idea. He rang him, as his contact details were on the paper with Andy's, the paper he had yet to destroy.

"Hello, am I speaking to Detective Inspector Harry Harper?"

"Yes, who is this?"

"The Prime Ministers private secretary, I am on route to a Mr. Andrew McIntosh, can you meet me there?"

"Your who?"

"I will be there within 15 minutes, I really need you there!"

"Why and how did you get my number or his address."

"The Prime Minster asked me to meet with you both, now please attend, there isn't much time."

Harry was now in panic mode, and rushed past Roger to his car,

"Sorry Rog have to go. Back later."

"Ok, thanks for sharing." Replied a surprised Roger.

Then Roger asked the desk sergeant,

"What is it with him, in the past week, he's been like my wife at that time of the month!" he paused, "It's not that, so maybe he's pregnant!"

"Well that's nice, hope your both be happy!" the sergeant joked.

***

20 minutes later Harry arrived outside Andy's and pulled up alongside a black BMW,

"You must be the Prime Ministers secretary; you didn't tell me your name?"

"John, call me John. Now we need to speak with Mr. Andrew McIntosh."

"Why? What's going on?" and rang the bell.

"I will explain once we're inside, I really need a cup of tea, the drive up is so long."

"You drove all the way?" replied a surprised Harry.

"Yes, had a police escort out of the city." replied John.

"Police escort! It's urgent then!" enquired Harry.

"Shall we go in." as the gate opened.

They both drove in. John made sure his car could not be seen from the road.

Andy was surprised to see Harry, but even more surprised to see John, who he remembered from his trip to see the PM in London,

"What have I done to deserve this honour. I'll make some tea. Hope you are well Detective Inspector Harper and you also Mr. Secretary, I trust the Prime Minister is well also?"

"Yes, I am well. I'm quite parched after driving up here."

Harry was getting impatient and asked,

"Look obviously the PM sent you about something urgent, as my meeting with him was top security, not even you were supposed to know, so what is it?"

Andy gave them their teas and led them to the sitting room,

"I have a horrible feeling I can answer that!" replied Andy.

"You!" questioned Harry Harper, and John smiled at his intuitive mind,

"Yes, me, Detective Inspector. I asked John if he was well and the PM, he only replied for himself. Also, the PM would not send his personal secretary up unless one thing!"

"What?" quizzed Harry.

"He's dead!"

"Don't talk crap I'm a police officer, I think I would have heard before most."

There was silence until John spoke,

"Normally yes, Inspector," replied John, "but on this occasion, no one else does know, yet! There will be a press release later today."

"Fucking hell! How." Muttered Harry

"Plane, unsure of details yet. Other than he left an instruction for me to meet with you two gentlemen."

Harry then asked,

"Terrorist attack, or plane malfunction."

Andy then added,

Plane malfunction is unlikely so, my money is on terrorist attack, but it could also be home grown attack from his latest actions ... which ... "

"Which what?" asked Harry. "Come on Andy, I know you are Mr. A."

John then confirmed it,

"Yes, he is! That's why I am here. The Prime Minister felt you two should work together as you both have certain talents. He also said if you were to bring to justice the perpetrators, that the Mr. A. file was to disappear."

"WHAT! I'm a copper, I'm supposed to arrest him, not work with him!" exclaimed a frustrated Harry.

John smiled at Harry's straight forward reply,

"Yes, I know your feelings Inspector, but you see the PM also had a hunch who was behind this. MI6 gave him some information on a hit, and it wasn't foreign but closer to home. Persons who we had not touched but were afraid he may be soon."

Andy felt as though the world had collapsed, in seconds his success with the PM had gone. Now he was known by them, and the police. The PM who was making changes, was now gone. It was like being back at stage one all over again.

"Who is this person, or group?" asked Andy.

"Before I divulge that, I need conformation from you, that you will both work together, and obviously this will have to be covert. Inspector you must be seen to do your normal duties, but no one else within the police must know. As for you Mr. McIntosh, you are well versed in covert operations, so a lot of the time you will be on your own. However, I will do I what I can to help. You may be surprised at what I can do for you, when given enough warning!"

Unbeknown to them Andy had on him a digital recorder, and had taped everything, as he did when he met the PM. It made sense to have insurance, he had always been a careful man, and planned for the unexpected.

"Covert is second nature to me, but I need more information, names, addresses, anything you have on anybody."

He was handed an envelope which contained papers, and a CD by John

"All you need is in here, take it and take several days to digest it before acting on anything, longer if needed. There is a direct line to me which I can scramble, trust no one else. Now I suggest we leave, I need to get back, and the Inspector can spend the next few days to catch up on his more mundane police work that I'm sure he has ignored since chasing the elusive Mr. A! Meantime, you Mr. Mcintosh digest the information in the file. I have also arranged for you to be at a formal evening function, many of the people that will be there are, on the list in that file. Your alias name and details are in there too, study them. It's a black-tie function obviously, so get a tuxedo unless you already have one. I will say goodbye now gentlemen . . . good luck."

They left, and Andy sat at his desk, and opened the envelope. Inside there was near fifty pages, and a CD. He started to scan the pages, first was a list of names, the following pages were of each person's details plus photograph, and a brief history, each stamped Top Secret.

Later that day he used the direct line to John to test him out, and to check that the line worked. As he waited for the phone to be answered, the line seemed to be clean, nothing cutting in such as listening devices.

"John, it's Andy go secure!"

"It already is."

"Can you get me supplies such as arms?"

"No! That type of thing can be traced, as I am sure you are aware, but I can tell you where to go. A man of your means can break in given a detailed copy of the location of certain

MOD buildings. I will post it to you, as Emails can be traced, sometimes the old ways are still the best!"

"Thank you for your confidence in my abilities, however John, MOD sites tend to be well guarded, and not by amateurs."

"I am aware of that. But I may be able to arrange a power cut, total black out to help. I have only one man I can trust these times, who could do this."

"Nice thought, but they all have backup generators on site."

"That's why I will make sure my man poses as a contractor who goes in to service the back up and supply you with a night blackout. Just give me a date, after you have seen the plans. Will send first class today personally."

***

A few days later Andy received an A4 envelope with copies of the plans of a military base, where he could get his supplies, Andy studied the layout, which tended to be similar on most bases. The hours passed until the clock showed that it was time for him to get changed for the high society function. The party where he would have to mingle with nearly half the people on the list. He had memorized his new identity arranged by John, fortunately he had kept it simple, with Andy posing as a security expert and owner of a large company which deal in security solutions, like his old company. He arrived at the grand country house in Oxfordshire, with its long gravel drive and stone lions either side of the front door. A man greeted him at the door, and ran a body scanner over him, to check for metal objects,

"I do apologise Sir, but everyone has to be checked, since the recent murders of high-profile members of our society."

"Carry on! I'm in the same line of business, so I'm used to it."

On hearing Andy's accent and line of business, the man relaxed a little,

"One of us then, ex-military I dare say, I'm ex services too. Para's. This lot in here have been shitting themselves. I hear they call the guy, Mr. A. They want his head on a plate."

Then some more guests approached, and the man changed his manner, and winked at Andy,

"Thank you, Sir, you may go in now. Again, my apologies for the inconvenience."

"That's no problem." Andy handed him a twenty-pound tip, adding.

"I trust everyone is following etiquette tonight and giving you the standard twenty-pound tip?" and winked!

"Oh! Indeed, Sir they are! I'm most grateful."

With that, the people waiting behind in their fine clothes all started fumbling for twenty-pound notes, much to the amusement of Andy and the glee of the security guard.

Inside a Glen Miller style band were playing in the large function room, just to the left of the entrance hall, where many people were gathering and mingling. Andy fancied a traditional ale, but at these functions it was wine, cocktails and egos. The women eyeing each other up to see who had the most expensive dress, or jewelry. Meanwhile the men compared medals and status. Andy stayed on fruit juice but implied to anyone it had Vodka in it. As the night drew on, more and more fell for the charms of the alcohol and loosened up. Some lost the silver spoon in their mouths, others became course and some the ability to walk the catwalk. Some of the ladies acted like cats, and the claws came out. Andy decided to

135

find the toilets to make room for a few more fruit juices, and also to use it as an excuse to get lost and snoop around.

He quietly opened a door and heard moans of lust, quietly coming from a table. On it lay a young attractive brunette, with her dress up to her waist, exposing her suspenders and stockings. A much older man in a Colonel's dress uniform, was working up a sweat, making her rhythmically move back and forth on the table as she moaned. Andy closed the door quietly and headed further up the hall, until he met an attractive older woman in her late forties, who obviously looked after herself, and was more sober than most. She asked Andy,

"Good evening, I'm trying to find my husband, he went off to find the little boy's room, and to show my daughters friend the ladies. I do believe he's got lost. Have you seen a Colonel with a full head of grey hair near here?"

He smiled and pointed to the room where he had seen such a couple. Andy carried on down the corridor and a few moments later world war three started in that very room. Andy turned and muttered to himself,

"That's nothing to what awaits you Colonel."

He was the lap dog of a General, who gave the others a bad name, and was responsible for giving the wrong advice, on which the PM acted. His motives were at times political, involved bribes, and at other times he just didn't care. Having lost his devotion to duty and country years ago. There were crooked politicians, judges, and lawyers with funny handshakes. There were some top council officials who earned more money than the PM, for doing less work than a road sweeper. They came in all shape and sizes, except for egos, which were all overflowing with self-importance.

Andy was finding the experience sickening; he had never seen so many rotten apples in one basket. There were only a handful of decent people there, and he found it odd that they all shared one detail in common. For some reason, those who had risen through the ranks, got there by being ruthless and selfish. It was amazing how much he was finding out, just by listening in on their conversations as the booze lubricated their mouths and brains. He was enjoying being sober and finding that they offered information so readily with the aid of alcohol, to a man they thought was one of them. On the inside of his pocket he had his trusty digital recorder going all night, with a tiny microphone fed under his lapel.

At the end of the evening, people started to leave stumbling out into the moonlight and the waiting limousines. Some had decided to have a dip in the fountain in the middle of the drives island, where all the lavish cars and chauffeurs waited patiently in line. It was at this point he twigged why so many rotten apples were at the party. It looked very much like they all belonged to a masonic lodge, he wasn't sure which one, but that didn't matter. As far as he was concerned most were living on borrowed time. So, he smiled and said his goodbyes, whilst thinking, 'enjoy it while you can gentlemen'.

Chapter 14

The following day Andy spent planning the first two hits. His plan now was two hits every second day. With the loss of the PM his future, and plans were uncertain, although from John he had knew allies in the upper ranks, he had to up his game. He contacted John and arranged for the raid on the MOD site for two nights time at 8pm. Until then he followed the target, making notes of their car parking habits, and of location of office, and home.

Come the night of the MOD raid, dressed all in black, he made his way to the site under a moonless sky. It was cold, with a mist setting in, not a night to be out. Dew was forming on the grass, which made it slippery under foot, his breathe forming mist in the cold damp air. With speed he cut through the fence. The section was away from the road, and in the shadows, with only the sound of the odd car passing in the distance, and an owl, perched in a silver birch tree looking on at Andy's progress. John's contact had come through with the power cut, which also cut out all CCTV. Now he was working on the generator, which he convinced them, was saturated with water from the damp conditions. Giving him reason to pull it apart, with a frantic soldier looked on, until the sergeant took over. Fortunately, he was none the wiser and said,

"Well this is the first bit of excitement I've had since the Middle East."

"Really!" came the reply from the maintenance man.

"Yes. Nothing ever happens here, who would be mad enough. Too many locked doors, and no signs telling you where to find anything of value, you'd need a map!"

"Well I should have it back online in half an hour."

"Good, because otherwise I'd have a situation." Replied the soldier.

"Situation?"

"Yes, the kettle wont bloody work without power!" the soldier laughed.

Meanwhile Andy had avoided one guard and was on his way to the Armory. John had supplied him with the code for the lock, and it worked. Andy went in and found the shelves empty!

He spun round and headed out. He'd been set up, or something had gone drastically wrong. Outside he heard footsteps racing his way, he hid in the shadows as two soldiers raced past him, then he started running to the hole in the fence. As he reached a corner another soldier appeared, who he quickly disarmed and made unconscious. Another appeared and ran past to help his colleague as Andy hid once more in the shadows, then came up from behind and put him down too, making sure neither were badly hurt. He then raced to the hole, whilst being chased by two men in dark suits. However, Andy was too quick, and dived through the hole, and disappeared into the darkness. Only an owl saw him in the dark, leaving the men bewildered.

***

The following day, Andy woke to the sound of the phone ringing, it was Harry,

"We have a problem, John the PM's secretary, has been found dead, and they are pinning it on you! There was a second body of a guy with fake ID and clearance for MOD Property. Both were in a car with gunshot wounds, although it was obvious, they were not shot in the car. Mr. A is being blamed for both, we need to meet and talk."

The agreement was to meet in a café at 10am, Harry was there first and saw Andy approaching. As he crossed the road to the café, he helped an elderly woman to cross. It showed that Andy was not all bad in Harry's eyes, he smirked as the little old lady shook Andy's hand and smiled. He wondered what she would say if she knew who her Samaritan was. Also, how long would it be before Mr. A's identity became common knowledge, stopping him from doing such deeds. The Policeman inside him was saying arrest and take him in, before the hole he was in got deeper, and out of hand. The amount of laws he had seen broken and been involved in were many. Andy crossed the road to the café. Harry looked him up and down using his policeman's gut instinct to analyses him. His one side calculated murderer, other side said that the ones Andy had killed were no better than the crooks he chased every day, except they had been getting away with it for years, with money and power on their side.

Andy entered, and held the door open so that a Mother with a pushchair, and toddler in tow, could get out first. Andy sat at the table and Harry thought to himself, is he an avenging angel, or a murderer. Then Harry gave him the news once more in detail in whispered conversation,

" …It also proves to me that some people on high want you badly, and that John's office was bugged. As a policeman, I should arrest you now, and take you in. But there is also the common man in me that sees you for what you are and see what you're trying to achieve. But I have to say Andy, I cannot, and will not put you above my career and the law. I could end up losing everything, and be in prison too, or if not shot like John." He looked into Andy's eyes, searching for answers and waited for a reply. Usual chatter of the café filled the void.

"I know that, that's why I think you should back off. What John and the PM had in mind was a nice idea, but not workable. If you could keep them off my back as much as possible, until I have arranged things with my house. But don't put yourself at risk." said Andy, and Harry whispered in reply.

"I will do what I can. I suggest you also do something about your bank, and movement of money. Transfers and ATM's are traceable, cash isn't, unless they are new notes, so be careful. How did your party go?"

Andy smiled with raised eyebrows,

"Never seen so much crap dressed up as sweet violets, although there were a few nice people."

Harry nodded and understood what he was trying to say, but added,

"Don't forget Andy, there are many trying to do what is right for the greater good."

"I know, sadly mud sticks and sours good intentions."

As Andy left the café Harry watched and saw the articulate part of him, which was full of dreams, wanting a better world to be born.

CHAPTER 15

On his return home Andy started his preparations, he had large waterproof flight case containers, in each he put fresh clothes. Two weapons, bivouac, tinned food with tiny opener, folding cutlery set, torch. £5000 cash and other items along with a silicon bag to ensure it stayed dry. He made three of these up and took them out just after dark and buried the flight cases at strategic places. He also moved money to an offshore account, and £20,000 in cash. Much later, he went straight to the village where he hoped to see the young Mother and child once more. He sat patiently on a bench, his mind mulled over his next hit, a Colonel. He hated the thought of a Military Officer, taking bribes and being mixed up in situations that saw the deaths of fellow comrades in arms. There were also stories that he may have been involved in abuse of young squaddies, but there was no evidence. It was possibly covered up to save face. After all, stories such as those could damage recruitment figures. Just as he was venturing into the dark depths of his soul, a light was switched on as he saw the Mother, and child appear from around a corner. It brought a smile to his face, as the scene reminded him of his own family cruelly taken from him. He approached her as she was about to go into the bakers. It had a small seating area, where people had coffee or tea.

"Here let me get the door for you, I think I did this yesterday!"

She looked at him, and as soon as she remembered, a warm smile lit up her face and made Andy forget about his troubles,

"That's kind, thank you. I remember now, I was struggling with my pushchair and the little one. I'm Jane."

"I'm Andy. Easier when your husband is with you, but we all have to work and put bread on the table." He looked at the bread shelves and smiled at his pun.

"Yes quite!" she laughed and stretched her back giving an indication it ached from walking, and pushing the child who was asleep.

"Forgive me" remarked Andy, "But you look shattered, I was about to buy a coffee here, would you like to join me and rest a while?"

Although he was a stranger, it was a public place which made her feel safe, and she could not resist the thought of a coffee and a chair.

"That's very kind of you. Pushing this little man and carrying shopping does make my back ache."

"I know too well!" said Andy

"You have family too?" she asked

Andy paid for the coffees and they sat down at a table. At another table was an old couple who smiled at the sight of the sleeping baby. On another table was a man dressed in a suit reading the Financial Times, and at another was a man in scruffy work overalls reading the local paper, while his work mate browsed the internet on his mobile. They both took a sip of coffee then Andy asked,

"What's the little man's name?"

"Ben, named after his Dad. What about your family?"

He went onto tell her the whole story. They were halfway through their coffees by the time he had finished, it was then he realised that this was the first time he had actually unloaded his thoughts to someone.

"That's my story! What of you and your family?"

"Sadly, my husband Ben, was killed 3 years ago. He was in the Navy. He and his team whilst killed when dealing with drug smugglers, not a common occurrence by all accounts, but my Tom was never one to shy away from doing his duty. He wore a body armoured vest, but a knife wound to the upper leg crippled him, he bled out quickly. He never even got to hold our son, who was born just two weeks after he sailed. I don't know why I'm telling you all this, we are strangers!"

"Because I understand maybe!"

Andy suggested a pot of tea, and she excepted, they sat down at a small round table, with the child asleep in the pushchair.

Andy suddenly felt the pain of empathy he had not felt in years. He then told her of his wife and child,

"So, you see we have much in common." Andy said in a comforting voice.

They both went on to talk about the Army life, the good and the bad.

"I still hear from his colleagues that survived, such a lovely bunch. It's true they are a second family. We try and meet up each year, family days. Last time I saw them, they told me about their Captain, a lovely man."

In his mind he thought of his team who were now all dead, and the hit made even more sense, because several on that list were heavily connected to the drugs trade,

"Which brings me to a favour I want of you," said Andy.

Instantly she looked concerned, to which Andy reacted,

"It's OK. It's nothing funny! You see I had a business and saved money to send my kids to a good school, and I would like to help you. I lost my family, and want to help another, and seeing you the other day reminded me of my wife and two kids. If not school, then just to improve your lives a little, it's what my wife would want me to do. I would only blow it on something stupid. So please?"

Completely stunned Jane was unsure what to do or say,

"I am, so sorry you lost your family. but I don't know you, and why would a perfect stranger do such a thing?" she asked.

"Because I am the lucky one. I came back from my tours of duty alive, whereas your husband didn't! Maybe it's my way of thanking God, or maybe because it's simply the right thing to do."

She sat stunned, but had a feeling that Andy could be trusted. He handed her the briefcase with the £20,000 in it.

"In here is a lot of money, cash, do you have a bank account?"

"Well, yes, but!"

"No buts. We will go now and put the money into your bank account. I just ask that you spend it wisely and bring that little one up well and enjoy every moment."

At the bank, the tellers were shocked at the amount of cash, Andy told them he had come into money and wanted to help a friend. He couldn't tell the real reason that he didn't want it traced. Meanwhile, Jane sat on a chair feeling faint after seeing so much cash,

"I'm dreaming, this only happens in the movies!"

She became emotional as they were leaving the bank and threw her arms around him,

"Did this just really happen or, am I dreaming?"

"It's real." Said Andy

"You are an angel."

They hugged, and Andy asked for her address, so he could write. She did so because he had no family at all, she felt sad for him. After parting he went to a solicitor and had a will made up, leaving his house to her. It helped him a sense of worth and facing reality that his days were numbered. Now more than ever, he didn't fear death, but he was determined to try and leave a better world behind, a better Government, with integrity and at least help one small family.

That night he slept soundly, and when he woke the next morning, he focused on the task ahead. He started to execute his carefully planned day. The hit was a Colonel Banner, with his friend, who was also on the list. Mr. Hyde-White MP and Colonel Banner were both playing golf on their usual course. A detail Andy had picked up at the party, in fact the party had supplied him with nearly all hit locations. He sat in an oak tree, with the rifle, and a high-power scope, which he had used before, but now Jimbo was dead, he was not going to be able to get any more ammunition, so one shot was the order of the day. If he could manage one shot with each target on the list, then he would have enough. He sat looking through the telescopic sights, until both men came into view. It took an hour until they appeared at the 6th hole. There was no one else around as Hyde-White presented the Colonel with an envelope, which Andy focused in on. It was cash, a lot of cash. What was it for? Andy didn't know, or care, as far as he was concerned the way it was given, and location, made it smell of something illegal. He took aim at the Colonels head and a split second later a robin landed on the rifle barrel. Was this a message from his wife to stop, God calling for peace, or was it simply Santa Clause passing through. Whatever it was, it made him pause long enough for the clear shot to vanish, as the two men started to walk the green once more.

One hundred yards more and the clear shot would vanish, he wanted them to stand side by side, one shot to kill both. Then by luck they both stopped. It looked as they were having a heated discussion, facing each other in line with Andy's rifle barrel, he squeezed the trigger. The silencer made a sound of a gentle thud, and the bullet flew. It made the Colonels head explod. Splattering blood over Hyde-White as his head gaped open as it received the same bullet. It sent his brain shooting out of his skull and landing on the ground. His body joined the Colonel's on the floor in a crumpled mess, blood spurting out, a few jets turned into a constant flow of dark red liquid, soaking into the green.

Andy kept looking to ensure no one else was about to come into sight, before he left the tree, but then through the sight he saw movement in some bushes at the side of the course. He prayed it wasn't young boys who would sneak onto the green to collect golf balls, to sell back to the wealthy golfers. The bush rustled some more as a fox appeared, it could smell the blood. It ran out, sniffed around the body, then picked up the brain, and ran back from where it came. Andy muttered to himself,

"The wolf is out to get you all."

Chapter 16

Andy slept lightly, as one of his nightmares returned. His family, were locked up in a brick block house, with only an air vent, through which he could hear their calls for help. He was bare foot, and hot coals surrounded the block house. He tried the door, his feet burning, a smell he knew too well from seeing his friends blown up and burnt. The door was locked and on it had the number 10. The numbers were white hot. He tries the doorknob which burnt his hand. His face was cracked and dry, from the scorching heat. He quickly steped back with his clothes in flames, he looked at his burnt palm. On it are numbers in a circle, three sixes' the sign of the devil. He screamed as the flames lapped up to his chest, as he breathed, the scorching heat, and flames, burned his throat and lungs. Looking at his palm, the numbers were turned around and read, three nines. He thrashed about in frustration trying to dowse the hot flames. He woke with a violent shake and sweat rolled down his face, the bed was wet from nightmare city. In the bathroom he drank from the tap.

Then using both hands, he splashed water over his head and ran his fingers through his hair. Staring at his reflection of salt and pepper hair, and eyes with crow's feet. Their sparkle was replaced with thin blood shot veins in the corner of each eye, and eyelids heavy with years of restless nights.

At his desk he fed his password into his laptop, the family picture last taken, graced the screen as a wallpaper. The list popped up, with the files John had given him of each 'suspect', a word used rather than 'target', so to give Andy a choice of public ridicule, law courts or elimination. As far as Andy was concerned the courts were bent, as with much of the law system, when a big name and wealth was involved. Public ridicule was for only those that could possibly change, and were not bad to the core. So far, only one had entered that category. Next on the list was another MP who before entering politics was a very successful industrialist. The politician was of new stock, a self-made millionaire, with many enemies, who attracted Andy's keen eye. On the road to wealth he trod on many toes, destroyed many small companies swallowing them up. In several cases he moved the companies out of the UK, to where sweat shops were the norm, and health & safety was none existent. The UK work force were left bewildered at a time when the company had been doing so well. But bigger profits swept their livelihood's away. The strength of the pound plus rising costs, were blamed was a spin story often used.

It earned him the nickname 'The Firminator'. His wife was quiet lady, once commanded all men's eyes to admire her perfection. Her innocence was to be drained by this man, with few human values. He could charm the birds out of the trees, then once down on the ground, he would pounce like a cat with claws that sliced through all legalities. Choking every last breath from all that came within his shadow, ready for the final kill. Now the tables would be turned.

***

The press was having a field day now on the killings of Mr. A, the one tabloid called 'Mr. Death', and, 'Most Wanted'. A title that was to die a death, as Mr. A, took the limelight and everyone in the media was using the title. There was a part of Andy that hoped the media would see his reasoning, his aim, but the media was owned by such people who were on the list of corrupt figure heads. As he saw it, at the top of the apple tree were the generals, some were rotten, souring the other fruit. As one came down the tree to the workers, and soldiers, the apples were well trodden to make cider for the rich. The others pushed down to the bottom of the cannon barrel, to become cannon fodder.

It was those thoughts that made him strive forward with his crusade. To rid the tree of all rotten fruit, and make way for the new blossom of the new age.

***

The following day he was up at 4am, just before sunrise, and waited outside the MP's house. A man, Mr. Fowler MP, who's daily routine was mapped out by Andy in the days after the party. He wanted every target with a daily routine mapped out, and their route to work, he did not want to waste months analyzing them, just hit hard and fast. He knew Harry's days were numbered, and it was only a matter of time before Harry was replaced with someone else, with shoot first policy. The security services would be a force to reckon with, and 'God forbid,' his old regiment

The birds started singing their morning song as Andy looked through his rifle scope from a brow of a hill, roughly 700 meters away. He didn't want a too longer distance between him and the target, to lower the risk of innocent beings, even animals getting in the way. He had seen too many innocent bye-standers get hit, because of the shooter being too far, and too low. The lights of the house had been on for half an hour as the front door opened. The target, Fowler came out into the sun e light, which came from behind Andy, he could see his wife behind him, and saw what resembled a more than heated discussion between them. He turned his back on her as she burst into tears holding a letter in her hand. Dressed in a classy silk night dress and matching gown, the middle-aged blonde held in her other hand a framed family picture. She had all the hallmarks of a down trodden trophy wife, who was about to be exchanged for a new model. She slowly shut the door, and tried to compose herself as Mr. Fowler MP reached his car. Andy had a clear, shot but decided that the woman did not need to see it, so he waited. His car left the drive, and drove towards Andy, up the old Roman road. Like all old Roman roads, it was nice and straight. Andy was sure he would put his foot down, and he did.

The BMW roared up the road as though in a race, but a race to his grave. Andy took aim just ahead of the car and squeezed the trigger, thud! The bullet left the silencer of Andy's rifle. It shot its way through the air to the windscreen of the driver's side. It was quickly followed by a second. The first smashed the windscreen and hit the targets neck and the jugular. Blood spurted over his white shirt and suit. His eyes were wide with shock and as if he was about to say 'what the f . . .' the second went through his mouth, and out the back. His cream leather back seat turned red, with pebble dashed brain-matter spattered all over it. The rear window was deco-rated in lines of blood, as the car swung to the right and into a hedgerow. The airbag deployed, blood spurting like a fountain all over it. The bag kept the body near upright for a few sec-onds, until his head fell forward exposing the gaping hole at the back of his head.

Andy calmly got up and left to the go to the next target, who lived only 45 minutes away. Andy carefully worked out the logistics of each hit, making sure the pair lived near each other.

***

Meanwhile, Harry, was just rising from his bed as his phone rang, it was his superior,

"Detective Inspector Harry Harper?"

"Oh, come on Tony, you know it's me. We've known each other since college days, or am I in trouble?" replied Harry.

"No Harry not in trouble, you know I have your back, but I'm afraid this Mr. A...business is...well it's been taken out of our hands as they want him fast. They are going via the back door, if taken alive there won't even be a jury."

"The law doesn't work that way Sir, trial by jury!" insisted Harry.

"Dead men don't require a jury. Come on Harry you know what goes on and is kept out of the public eye. If they want you gone, it's goodbye!" came the reply.

"When is this 'take over' taking place?" asked Harry

"As from 1am this morning, they don't sleep Harry."

"Who are they? Are we talking MI6, MI5, or one of the other cloak and dagger brigade?" Harry asked.

"I don't know and don't want to know. If you must know it was the Home secretary." Came the final solemn reply.

Then the telephone conversation ended, leaving Harry concerned for Andy, until he heard on the radio that an MP had been found dead in his car, under suspicious circumstances. He knew it was Andy, and that it meant he was still on the road, or in hiding. Andy by now was lying in wait for the Industrialist Millionaire, outside his country retreat, with his lover, while his wife, up in Halifax, thought he was in London on business, not the Cotswold's.

This time, due to trees, hedges and proximity of the house close to others, there was no clear field of fire. His mobile started to vibrate an incoming text, it read,

'Been taken off case, the wolves are out, watch your back. Don't go back to house, now being watched. This is sent to you via a throw away mobile bought cash, so can't trace. Like the old westerns its's Dead or Alive. Sorry but you're on your own now. Do not reply to this mobile as it will be ditched. I am sorry, H.'

Andy thought it would come to this, that's why he sited 3 boxes with the required gear. The target came out of the house and set off in his car, closely watched by Andy from a distance. As the car drew near, Andy picked up a remote-control console, at his side that controlled a large electric model car with its body shell replaced by plastic explosives, and a mobile phone as a detonator. He thought he would try to improvise on the spot to throw the police, or who-ever, off the track, by putting the blame at the lover's door. Although he knew they would soon work out it wasn't her, but it might buy him a day, or two. He had managed to obtain the house land line phone number of where he had just left, with his mistress sipping earl grey tea. He phoned it,

"Hi is that Suzie?"

"Speaking!"

"John just rang me from his spare business mobile to say his usual number has just died on him. Can you call him on this number, he needs a number from his directory on his desk? He needs it quick as his car just broke down and needs to call these people to tell them he will be late."

"Why didn't he just call me rather than you?"

Quickly he came up with a reply to the sticky question,

"To let me know he would be late for our meeting with these gentlemen, and his battery was low and wanted to save the power for calling the number, he wants from you to call the breakdown. Just give him the number quickly and don't stay chatting, as he's panicking about his battery life. He said he had such a good time last night he forgot to put the thing on charge. Must have been a hell of a party!"

He could almost feel her blushing over the phone.

"OK" and she did. With Andy wishing her to hurry up as the car drew nearer. She got the desk directory ready and was calling the number as Andy controlled the car which came out from a field entrance ahead of him. As Johns car made its way along the country lane, Andy brought the remote model car underneath it, and kept up with it waiting for the phone call. His mistress was phoning as the car got nearly level to where Andy was positioned in some trees. But she misdialed and started again as the car passed underneath with the bomb. Andy struggled to keep the bomb laden model car up with its bigger cousin. Andy thought his plan to shift blame was a bad one. She dialed again, the mobile was waiting to receive the signal, as a corner came up. The BMW with the bomb, raced underneath, and started to go around and out of sight. Then split seconds later the phone detonator got the signal. Boom! The loud explosion ripped through the car, making the petrol tank explode in a spectacular fashion, with colours that matched the sunrise.

Andy made his escape quickly, very shortly people would be reporting it, there was a house was within hearing, distance and emergency services would soon arrive.

It wasn't long until he uncovered the first box full of kit hidden in a wood, and proceeded to errect a camouflaged small covering with a bivouac. He had left the car out of sight and sat under a tree reading through his notes for his next hit. After a few hours he listened to the local radio. A news-flash reported the first killing, which was confirmed as another 'Notorious Mr. A' hit. It then went onto say,

"He has been holding the country to ransom. If they do not make certain changes to policies quickly, to convince Mr. A. then more killings can be expected. We have obtained from a whistleblower, copies of the requests from Mr. A. The requests are topical, and have been many times the focus of several articles in the media, which highlighted the wasting public money, illegal wars, crooked politicians and public figures. He requests certain people be removed from office, and changes in political polices of the government. A full list will be published in tomorrow's papers. The government has made some changes, but not enough for Mr. A, as the changes seemed to stop with the death of the Prime Minister and his secretary. This, in itself, has the conspiracy theorists buzzing. The Deputy Prime Minister, clearly said in a public announce-ment, that they did not bow to terrorism. Yet we have seen them bow in the past to others where religious differences played a part, but maybe this one is too close to home. We shall see. As we have more details, we will report again."

***

A short while later there was another news item on the death of the industrial millionaire, but not linked to Mr. A. It stated that the mistress was helping with their enquiries. Which meant that within 48 hours they may have worked out that she was innocent, and that the man was on Andy's list. Maybe it would occur to them because the PM making the changes had been assassinated, all bets were off. Mr. A's efforts could now escalate. These were conversations his mind he was having with himself, he tried to cover every angle and near future outcome of recent events.

Andy switched the radio off to conserve power, he hoped to see changes or hear news from the new guy at the top, but his guts said no. He set trip wires around his position which he would attach to his big toe, a simple warning system that was affective, even though old fashioned. Darkness fell and Andy lit up his watch. It was 1am, and he couldn't sleep, he was restless. Whether it was worry of his situation or afraid of falling asleep, then falling victim to nightmares, that still regularly haunted him.

Suddenly he felt a slight tug on his big toe, then another stronger one. He slowly and quietly grabbed his knife to cut the string, freeing his toe, then peered outside of the shelter. In the pale moonlight he followed the course of the trip wire. Then gradually he made out the shape of something moving in and out of the undergrowth, then another moving shape became three. Then there was scampering of feet, it was the four feet of a badger and two cubs. Andy relaxed, smiled, and spent the next hour watching the mother play with her cubs. He hadn't been at peace in a long time, watching this carefree little family enjoy each other, made him envious. He thought how often do we open our eyes and see the simple enjoyments that surround us. Humanity was caught up in the digital age of fast communication and fast living. But no warmth of heart, technology with its learning from a machine, and not a book. Ruling bodies that saw money and position, not the souls and people they served. What did the future hold for us all?

The next morning, he woke after only a few hours' sleep, but felt very much alive. Watching the badger and her cubs in the cool night air under a mellow moonlight, calmed him so much, that when he did sleep, he did not dream, he was just in a deep sleep.

He looked out at the damp morning dew, breathing in the sharp air that had a cutting freshness. There was a mild crisp frost on the ground, lighting up the woodland. He packed the gear away back into the watertight box, and covered it in freshly cut branches, then headed off to his next hit. On arrival he parked a quarter of a mile away, in some woods in Herefordshire, a county he knew quite well. He was about to leave the car when he had a call on his mobile, it was Harry,

"Yes Harry!"

"How did you know it was me?"

"No one else alive has this number now!"

"Not sure how to take that, sounds disconcerting. The team that's on your case are good, too good. They have your car details and put out a call on it. I dare say you have already fixed false plates on it, but with the systems we have today…It's only a matter of time, you best dump it."

"Message received and understood. Thanks Harry, this must be costing you a fortune in mobile phones, having to dump it each time we speak, so not to be traced,"

"Yes, so you owe me. One other thing, I don't know how long I can keep this up, as it goes against the grain, it's not what I am about. I'm a copper. I stand to lose a lot. Now, much of the media are against you, but there are some that are for you, and you have small support for what you are trying to achieve, but the public are fickle. Spin doctors are putting out fake news on you. Dodgy history and lies that are not pleasant at all. However, the minority reports are trying to clean that up and sort out the fake from the truth. You put one foot wrong, and you are damned,"

"I know, I'll be seeing you Harry, thanks for what you have done. Take care," Then the phone went dead, and Andy was on his own.

***

He made his way to the next target, another Politician who had his fingers in many pies, with conflicts of interest, considering his position. As a chairman of an arms manufacturer his constant trips abroad at the taxpayers expense gave him ideal opportunities to gain contracts for the company, who in turn paid a generous bonus. He was covered in more dirt than a pig farmer and smelt worse. A family man, who saw more of the bottom of a whiskey glass at his club, than he did of his family. Two boys at public school, who hardly ever went home, just one annual holiday abroad with their mother, who no longer lived with their father. She had turned to visiting nightclubs in search of companionship. Retro nights reminded her of better times, which her allowance made sure she always had funds to keep herself, and friends happy with drinks & food, plus enough to pay for a taxi home. Andy saw him as a waste of a man, he had everything that Andy once had, a family. But he was blind, blinkered and dazzled. Like a rabbit crossing the road, running in all directions, rather than the straight and narrow. He left what mattered behind and was lured by greed.

He had decided not to use his rifle on this occasion he was getting low on ammunition, so chose something old fashioned and simple. Through binoculars he watched as the man left his grand house drove down a gravel drive and out of the gates. For some reason unbeknown to Andy, it made him think of his own biological father, who he saw, worked himself into an early grave to support for his family. A proud man who would not take charity, brought him up strictly, which gave him good grounding for the armed forces. He found himself appreciating his father more now, than he did when he was alive, even though his actual father was dead by the time he was five, the memories were strong. His foster parents were of the same breed, strong and old fashioned. Maybe, this was because he had a family, or had been through so much, or simply because as he got older, he became wiser. He first noticed a change in himself when his children were born. He found himself repeating the things to them, that his father had once said to him. His father told him,

"Son. You will make mistakes, that's OK, but learn from them. I have made plenty, learn from mine too! Life is about moving forward, the next generation doing better than the one before. Remember that!"

As those memories echoed in his mind, he related it to his targets and the whole system. It seemed to him that the system didn't learn from past mistakes, there was still corruption, 'I'm alright Jack, you peasants can sod off!" attitude towards the average person.

Andy waited along the narrow single-track road that lead to the main road, which he used every morning to get to the train station. He was armed with a simple explosive device with a strong magnet. He walked at the side of the road, facing the direction that the targets car would come. There was a cool breeze and just for a moment he thought he could smell his father's aftershave, Old Spice. The car got closer, Andy pressed the fuse timer behind his back, and when the car came closely alongside, he quickly attached it, making look as though he had been clipped by the car. He shouted at the car, like any other person would, but started counting backwards instead shouting abuse. The car went on a short distance before the device exploded, closely followed by another explosion as the fuel tank went up, encasing the car in flames, and sending it up a hedge. Andy checked that no one was getting out from the burning wreck, then he disappeared back into the wood. From there he quickly went on to his next target, feeling slightly lightheaded. Staying away from major roads, and Police presence, as he knew they were, by now, looking out for his car. Therefore, he kept his targets within a ten-mile radius where possible.

Outside the house of his next target was an ambulance and crew bringing out a man, who, he could only assume was the mark, as he lived alone. Andy just wondered whether he had heard about his previous hit and suffered a heart attack, but it was too soon for the news to travel. So, he concluded it must be the child pornography he used to get his kicks, which had finally put strain on his evil heart. Were his actions driving people to have heart attacks? If so, then driving fear into them might help make reaching his objectives that bit easier!

The next four days at the rate of two per day, he assassinated a further eight, which fueled the media and movements within Government. Now the first two flight cases of supplies were exhausted, and he was on his way for his final night at his second flight case camp.

Driving back, he was passed a roadside café, where in the car park was an identical car to his, model and colour. He pulled in next to it, checked to see if anyone was about, then took out a small power-screwdriver from the glove box. Un-screwed the other cars plates and switched them with his making sure not to be seen. Then he put his old ones back on the other car. Just as he finished screwing the last screw, someone came into view from the café. Andy pretended to be tying a shoelace, and casually got up and walked back to his car, as the other person went to a van. He jumped back into his car and maneuvered out with the van in front of him. He knew changing the plates would only buy him a few days at best, but he was halfway through his list, and the Government according to the media had actioned on many of his requests, meeting him more than halfway on a few and all the way on many. Only one was left, but Andy felt a profound sense of achievement, but at what cost? For a short time, he had a purpose, but also knew that the last one may not be acted upon. Home politics was one thing, international was another, and a Mr. Parsons was a hatchet and ideas man, who gave bad advice to the powers that be. He lined his pockets at the cost of the public purse. However, there was one piece of information missing from Andy's file. He had an identical twin brother, who was blessed with the good genes, unlike the crooked Parsons.

***

On the morning that Andy waited for Parsons to appear from his house, the twin had been visiting his nephew and sister in-law. The crooked Parsons was not at home, but at his lovers. Andy patiently waited, through his sites he spied the twin leaving the house, believing it to be the other brother. He had a perfect high vantage point and view of the road, and junctions, with hedges freshly cut and low, giving a good line of sight. The twin kissed his sister in-law on the cheek and hugged the kids, making Andy think he was having one of his better days. Making himself look like the doting Dad before travelling to be with his lover or, to the office for more planning on destroying companies, and people lives. As Andy watched through the scope, he saw the twin leave in the silver car. He followed it through the telescopic sites, along the straight road that lay parallel between them. Up ahead Andy could see a crossroads where he would stop. There were two cars approaching the crossroads as the twin pulled up at the junction. Andy covered the trigger as he focused on the twin through the side window, who was waiting for the oncoming cars to pass. The first passed, but the second signaled to turn right into the twin's road, making Andy's shot unsafe. The car turned and for a few seconds Andy's shot was obscured, then the twin saw the open road, and pulled away from the junction.

As he drove away Andy fired. On doing so, he was making a huge mistake. That the evening news broadcasted the 'Murder of a good man'. Instantly his support dwindled to nil, and now he was the most wanted man. The crooked Parsons went into hiding and Andy found himself cut off. He was on his own, hated by all. He had little in the way of supplies, weapons and ammunition was in short supply, Harry was unable to help. His only nameless friend was the internet blogger who was trying to point out the possible mistaken identity, was not being listened to in earnest. Even Marion had gone quiet, as he was poison to everyone's career, anyone who tried to show any support, no matter how small. His face was in the media, every day, and each day the blogger tried to point out the possible mistaken identity. However much main media produced fake news was to further embellish the downfall of Mr. A. After all the people in charge of those groups thought they may be on his list. Much of this unbeknown to Andy, who now had no access to news, a few days later the blogger was silent.

***

Andy hid away in his fox hole for the next week, living off what supplies he had put aside. He even picked up roadkill, and cooked it over an open fire, which reminded him of old days with his troop. He could not use his mobile for fear of being traced. For the first time he felt lost, even though what he had been doing had been leaving a lasting effect. The rotten apples were disappearing, except for a few minor ones. These were now changed people, even Parsons had turned over a new leaf. The death of his brother left a scar, which would not heal. Every time he looked at his children, a sense of exhaustion and dread consumed his soul, as he realised the person that he had been. He was to blame for his twin's death, if he had been more like his twin, then this would never have happened.

The authorities had approached most of Andy's old colleagues, and friends, who all had the same answer that they had not seen him in a long time. Exaggerating the length of time to help Andy, give him a chance, but it was true that they did not have a clue of his whereabouts. Andy, still in his fox hole hideaway, was unaware of teams of men with dogs, searching woods and forests a few miles away. Experience told him. to move onto a new county, but on foot. Avoiding public view would not be easy, with full pack, he would have to stay off main roads, but as he rubbed his bristled chin, he contemplated the situation and remembered the pictures circulated of him in the press, showed him clean shaven, but now he was not. With a full beard, he decided to gamble on the fact he looked like a tramp, carrying his worldly possessions on his back. He had £3k in cash, a rifle he broke down to fit in his ruck sack along with some food, sleeping bag and gear to make a makeshift camp.

He set out to foxhole number three, and the third of the three flight containers he had buried. It was some hours before he came within sight of it, the containers were airtight so the sniffer dogs would not pick up any scent. But what he saw he was not expecting, a young couple getting very intimate. He decided to try and get back to his house, which was not too far away. There he had a motorcross bike and gear stored at his house. He knew he had access that the authorities may have missed at the back of the property. Once there, sure enough he found his way in. The main gates to the house were taped up and a new chain, and padlock fitted, but Andy sneaked his way into the garage, which was out of sight of the lone policeman at the main gates. He checked the bike had a full tank, then fitted false number plate that he had hidden. Taped to Miss August on a calendar, he winked at her as he removed it, revealing her ample assets. Previously he had also fitted a switch to isolate the rear light, in case of being followed at night, which would make plate ID impossible. He wheeled it down to where he came in. Thick ivy growth concealed a wooden door through a brick wall of the garden perimeter. It was a four/stroke bike so when starting, it was slightly quieter than most. He had already prepacked it with extra gear, just in case it was required. It was as though the police had not even checked the garage. The authorities had not yet gone through his house. So, making most of the opportunity he stored items in secret hiding places built into the property earlier. Many things where hidden there, so he would return, keeping his visit a secret, which was paramount and this, he had achieved.

He started up the bike, unnoticed in the distance by a policeman at the main gate and set off across fields. He followed tractor tracks to a field entrance in a lane, then onto a main road and into the next county Gloucestershire. He headed to a Major Young, a man he once served with many years ago, who he trusted. He pulled up at the back of the country house and knocked on the stable door. The elderly Major answered,

"I wondered how long it would take for you to turn up at my door!"

"How did you know it was me?" asked Andy

"I know my men, I know you. Now then, do I call the police, or do I let you use my stables, or the barn to sleep in. Maybe to use as a base for a few days?" the Major said in a commanding voice.

"I leave it to you Sir." And put his wrists out to accept handcuffs.

"Go on, the barn is free, and I will put the kettle on. You can then tell me what the hell is going on."

Then the old Major paused, turned and called back,

"Andy. You're a damn bloody fool to try and take on the establishment. There I've said it. Now, I'll put the kettle on, and we'll have a cup of tea."

After he finished stashing his gear away, he joined the major in the kitchen of the large old farmhouse, and then told him the whole story. Nearly an hour had passed with the Major absorbing every, detail and in the back of his mind, wondered how he could help.

"Andy that would make a good movie, but now you must sleep."

He directed him to a spare room and retired himself, but before doing so he had one other thing to say,

"Ok you killed some of the rotten apples as you poetically put it. However, my boy, you do realise that because you shot the twin by accident, the media will not see it that way. Your well intentioned 'cause', is irreversibly tainted and damaged. The media will tear your limb, from limb! Sleep well."

Chapter 17

The next morning, he had breakfast with the major and told him more of the story, including the part about Jimbo, whom the Major had known well. The Major played with his handlebar moustache and asked,

"I understand your reasons for such actions, but why? You told me last night of your cause and aims, but not what started this all. What ignited the fire that's burning inside that head of yours?"

"When I lost my wife Sarah, and my daughter, my life fell apart. Then my son died, with all hope gone, all because of a drunk at the wheel of a car. He hardly served any sentence at all because of a lawyer, and an idiot judge. Those who sit pretty in their palacious bubbles of 'I'm alright Jack'. He paused and sighed,

"I wanted to make things happen! The politicians are paid by the people to improve our lives. Yet many only want to improve their own. I saw corruption in the army too! It's everywhere! The rotten apples are few and I want to rid the tree of the rotten ones."

"I understand what you are saying Andy, but it's still premeditated murder. Assassination in the eyes of the law. A noble cause, in a mad way, but doomed to failure. You are attempting to take on the system, powers that be the institution. People in the past have tried and failed, Guy Fawkes! or, is that what you want? Because believe me son, that will burn you alive. However, on saying that, you have indeed made them change a great deal, but at what cost? The PM was evidently murdered with the plane mysteriously being brought down with all its crew, and aides. The rotten apples are out of the basket, but for how long. These people are devious, with a long reach, and will stoop to any level to achieve their goal. Which is simply power, wealth and greed? These people have the power to cover up your assassination and bury all your ideals, forgotten history."

"So, what do you suggest Major."

"A strong government is like a tree, an army regiment, each member or branch, that supports the next branch above. That is something you can't really guarantee. All you can do is set the foundations, but unfortunately the wolves are out for blood, because you shot the wrong man. Mud sticks, you need to make that mistake good. Mud washes away, but blood stains for a long time. You need the public opinion on your side."

"How? The people that I am in contact with in the media, I can no longer contact. Not without putting them at risk."

"I might be able to help there, but we will have to be careful. After all, I am harboring a criminal now, but there is one person I trust, that might be able to help."

"Who is that?"

"My son, he's a reporter specializing in war zones and countries with political unrest. One could say he is a chip off the old block! I fought, but he films, and records it. He has been abroad filming and I know he has taken a great interest in what has been going on here, although he doesn't know that it's you, or that I know you. He will want to meet you of course. He's due back tomorrow, for now you need to stay low and do not answer the door or phone."

"Thank you Major, but rest assured if things go pear shaped, then I will not put you, or your family in any type of risk, I will just leave."

"Either way Andy, you are a marked man. Your plan may succeed, but you will lose. No matter the reason, you committed murder."

"I know, I don't care. What I care about is that I can change things, before I move on and join my family."

It was now the Major could see how far Andy was willing to go, which made him dangerous and why the authorities wanted him eliminated. Apart from being an embarrassment, he was shaking the political world to its very core. Dying never used to worry Andy, but now he was embracing it. It was not IF the reaper came, but WHEN. He spoke with his son Tom who immediately said.

"Good God Dad, he is a wanted man! and not just your average on the run crook . . . But he's also the biggest story to hit the British media since Jack the Ripper. I could make a mini documentary on the guy and tell both sides of the story. But it could put me at risk for knowingly interviewing a criminal wanted not just the police but the secret service. However, on saying that it could also be a meal ticket for me, or it could ruin me! I heard off some colleague's abroad, that in a few countries there has been copycat incidents. He is becoming a world phenomenon."

"No news is bad news I suppose! But please son, show a sensitive balanced view."

"Of course I will. I will be with you by 10pm tonight, can I meet with him then?"

"Yes, no problem! Drive safe!"

**

The sun had gone down when Tom arrived at the old farm-house. That night, and for the next few days Tom came to know Andy and worked on a storyboard for a documentary style interview, which he would film himself, so as not to put anyone else at risk. His mind was in overdrive on the possibilities of the outcome. He set up in front of the inglenook fireplace, in which a small fire burned gently, giving a lovely orange and yellow glow to the scene. He placed a single spot lamp behind Andy's head which threw his face into dark shadow. Tom pointed out to Andy that people would be unable to see his face unless he leaned forward, where the fire would light up his face. But his voice would not be disguised unless he wanted it, Andy said no, as he wanted people to hear it from his heart, not a computer voiced version. Over Toms shoulder was the camera, and in between, out of camera shot was the microphone. Tom kept the questions simple, and let Andy tell the whole story, starting with the loss of his family.

Towards the end of filming, Tom had a better clear view of Andy's reasons and actions, but still didn't feel comfortable about cold blooded executions. Then Andy went on to explain, during which time Tom left the camera running as a candid shot.

"In the past this country has had civil war to make radical political change, the people didn't like the crown as they felt they had no voice, even though there was a parliament. Eventually the crown lost some power, and parliament gained, but then politicians started to abuse their position. It was their job to improve people's lives, but greed took over. An 'us and them', attitude took over and replaced the original views … well that's how I see it."

Tom quietly asked,

"But your reasons seem to go deeper, much deeper! Are you afraid to die?"

"No." came a quick response.

There was silence as they just stared at each other in a now chilled atmosphere. Even the open fire could not stop the chill Tom felt from the depths of Andy's eyes, whose face was now lit up by the flickering flames of the fire as he leaned forward, giving his beard face a menacing feel. Andy's tired eyes, almost vacant suddenly came alive and he leant a little more across to Tom,

"Are you afraid to die Tom?".

Tom's spine turned to ice and his mouth dried up, and he felt a quiver in his voice as he replied,

"I've been in many war zones filming, facing death!"

"Indeed, you have Tom. You've seen more than most. Certainly, more than the politicians that send the troops into a war zone. But I am only two feet away from you!" then he laughed.

"Look Andy I want to tell your story, trying to help, I don't need this threatening crap."

Andy leant back and smiled,

"Threatening crap? You and everybody put up with it every day in the media. The lies and corruption, fake news and false promises. As we fucking speak two dictators in two separate countries thousands of miles apart, who are the best of friends, running the countries into the dirt. Syphoning off the wealth, while the people are starved, murdered and treated like shit!"

The camera was still rolling as Andy raised his voice, it had a slight quiver hidden in its depths,

"You asked me if I am afraid to die. When we die, we go to heaven, that's where my family are waiting for me. I know I'm not going to hell."

"But people who kill go to hell, we are told?" Tom replied in a mellow voice.

"Another lie. No sunshine I won't go to hell, because this IS HELL ... where the meek are downtrodden and left to work till they drop, in a world full of despair and false promises. A place were world leaders and governments, turn a blind eye to truth and doing the right thing is considered political incorrectness, while they feather their own nests and careers. Throughout history the same thing happens, as though the people at the top learn NOTHING ... nothing!"

He paused and drew breath,

"We are all cannon fodder, slaves to a corrupt world that is rotten to the core."

He then focused his eyes on the camera. Tom was afraid he may switch it off, because this speech was raw, but it was gold TV ratings stuff, totally unrehearsed and from the heart.

"That's right rotten to the core. A is for apple and I am throwing out the rotten apples. A is for Andy. I am cleansing the corridors of power, and I will not stop until my work is done."

Tom saw classic documentary material, while the Major saw a broken man, a product of a broken system.

***

Tom stayed up all night editing and splicing in the music, for Andy's final rotten apple speech, he put in Adagio for Strings Op 11. To give it punch and gravity from the heart.

By 9am he caught the train and by midday Tom was showing the footage to a close friend, a woman who ran a TV program on world events and news. She was blown away.

"My God Tom this is not only the biggest news since Jack the Ripper, it is so powerful, it is pure gold. What's your price? Name it!"

Tom saw the excitement and a slight tear in her eye from listening to the footage,

"It's priceless, you can't afford it." Tom replied.

"What! Then why bring it to me." she asked.

"Because how do you put a price on justice and liberty. That's what he was fighting for, maybe we are not going to agree with it. But he, as he puts it, only picked rotten apples, except for one that was mistaken identity. A mistake, that he regrets deeply. No, there is no price high enough, that's why I am giving you a copy, and I'm going to give it to others too, free! That way you can't own it, and it can be shown by others. Everyone should see this. Many won't air it, but enough will. It's a story that should be told, that's totally unbiased and true. This is real, not fake news that floods the air ways today."

She stood back and shook his hand,

"I will air it tomorrow night, if you get the others to air it on other nights then you could have it playing for at least 3 days or more."

Andy was restless in the evening when the program started, and couldn't bring himself to watch it, but the Major was glued to it. Andy came in after the hour-long program had been on. Tom had created a sympathetic one-hour documentary, that withheld no punches. It told the truth, the reasons and more importantly showed dossiers on each victim's seedy past. Plus, it pointed out that the one man killed had been mistaken identity. Something that got washed over in previous news reports. That night, Andy's nightmares returned as he watched himself on TV talking of the past. Then present, brought back other memories.

For everyone else, the program finished with the final candid shot and Andy's ending speech.

Chapter 18

The following day all media focused on the program. Many people had not seen it, but it was on other channels that coming evening, and the media coverage was ensuring mass viewing. Advertising rate shot up during the programs airing. The media was now not so much anti Mr. A. In fact, reading between the lines, there was a hint of support. As the day drew on and people digested it more and more, they were seeing Andy's point of view. Some were on the fence, and some against his action, but they were now a minority. The corridors of power were in panic mode and the PM ordered Tom to be interviewed. In that interview Tom pointed out that he had not broken any laws, as he had not harbored him and that it had only taken an hour to make the film during which he never felt in danger, also public opinion would be on his side as making the film was in the public interest and the fact that he didn't do it for monetary gain. It was also fair to say, that many within government departments were even in favour of it but feared to admit to it. Tom was a respected name in his line of work and the arrest only added to greater advertising, and fueled the fire of support. The power of the press, being strangled by those above? This feedback got back to the Prime Minister who ordered a search of all places connected with Tom, including the Major's house. By which time Andy had already left clean shaven, and with dyed hair. He left an envelope of cash and a thankyou note for the Major, which he read with a smile then put in the fire, as he knew he would be visited by men in suits or uniforms very soon. They did later that day, but the Major did a wonderful impression of being vague and forgetful. Outside the Police searched the outbuildings and the woodland but found nothing.

Andy was now 10 miles away in his last hideaway foxhole and had his last remaining target on his mind. The folder was crumpled and dirty, but the information was clear. Target Miss Monique Jane, a stunning woman who had a varied past having had four careers, she worked up the corporate ladder to chief executive of a leading utilities company. She had the glamour of a Hollywood sex symbol, but the heart of the hardest cutthroat businesswoman, with the talent of breaking the opposition in business, and breaking lovesick hearts. By using her position, and her large salary, she invested in many small companies, except those companies that were fronts for seedy, and very illegal activities, including importing young women for the pleasure of men at their private clubs and in the cellar bars dotted around London and various large cities. Her idea was that no one would suspect a beautiful woman of such crime. The authorities knew of her, but there was little, to no proof, and several of the customers who visited these establishment held high positions in law enforcement and government. So, when they got wind of people asking awkward questions, they made sure questioning hit a brick wall.

They had too much to lose to let any investigation be carried out, that would affect their careers, and wives which could ruin them. At the bottom of the list was a case of murder, she had been accused of a hit, but due to lack of evidence it never even went to court. She was expert at manipulation of men, who were bewitched by her looks. Her long black hair, and even longer legs, topped up with an expensive breast enhancement. For many years she had taken pleasure in climbing the social league ladder, those who got in the way were soon sent tumbling down the ladder. She lived by a code in her business life, when it came to her competitors, 'Don't get mad, get even!'. That generally meant they lost everything, which included their moral standing within their community.

He stared at the file containing a picture of her and he felt a sense of unease, as he had never targeted the fairer sex. Even though the detailed file showed a person of dubious character, it still didn't rest easy with him. How could such a gorgeous woman be more evil than many others on his list. It made no sense. He thought of his wife and what she would be saying to him on his exploits to date, and now he was going to be killing a woman.

***

The sun had gone down, and dusk was turning into darkness, his eyes grew tired, and he lay back onto his sleeping bag and gradually he fell into a deep sleep full of bad dreams. In his dream he was looking at the woman through sites of a rifle. He followed her with the sites with his finger posed ready over the trigger. She was about to get into her car, and he squeezed the trigger. The bullet hit her in the back. She fell against the car slowly turning around showing a gaping hole in her chest,

177

but her face was not of Monique Jane, but of his beautiful wife Sarah mouthing his name.

He woke in a cold sweat and held his head in his hands and started to silently weep and tremble.

***

The sun rose, sparkling on the morning dew. After a while mist formed as the dew evaporated in the morning sun. Within an hour he was outside Monique's house where she lived alone. A Georgian style modern house that stood at the end of a long drive, away from the main road, known locally as millionaire's row. He parked under a tree on his motorbike and waited for her to leave, so he could follow and study her daily routine. He knew he could kill her on route to work, or in the home as she lived alone. But his heart told him not to, and just stand back and study her. Was it her slender fit looks, or was there more to her?

The front door opened, and she came out wearing a grey pencil skirt and matching jacket, carrying two small bunches of flowers. Sliding into her Porsche revealed plenty of leg and a barely black stocking top. She drove out and Andy followed. Andy was expecting to follow her to the city, but the Porsche came to a stop at a village church. She got out of the car and walked into the graveyard with the flowers. She approached two graves and put flowers on each. Through binoculars he could see her say a few words as she wiped a tear gently with her tissue from her immaculately made up face. He assumed they were her parent's graves, and when she returned to her car, he followed her to her place of work. He later watched her take her lunch break alone and return to work. This time he went into reception and cleverly pretended to be seeking employment. With his now younger looks, clean shaven, and with dark brown hair he engaged in small talk to the young, pretty, receptionist, and asked,

"I hear that the person in charge is called Monique Jane, is she the one I write to?"

"You can, or address it to Manager HR."

"Nice name, is she?" and winked.

"Actually, she is lovely to women but can be very stern with men. I suppose in high management she has to be!"

Andy took his time over this one as something didn't add up. He sat on a park bench that fortunately overlooked her office. He assumed she would not possibly leave until 5.30pm. So, at 5.15pm he started to walk up and down near the office, pretending to chat on his mobile phone. The time was now 6pm and Andy was sitting on his bike, along a side road waiting for her car to appear. It was 6.15pm. now he started to wonder where she had gone, as it looked as if all the staff had gone home. Through one window a cleaner had already started her shift, but then the familiar slender figure came walking out, as though on a catwalk. Carrying her briefcase with attitude in a seductive manner that caught everyone's eye whom she passed on the way to her car. She walked by one young man who could not resist turning on his pin-stripe tight skirt. Andy watched her get in her car, as she slipped into the seat, her skirt rose up. She closed the door then put on her glasses. She slowly reversed out of her private parking spot in front of the office, which bore name plate, and drove off. He started to follow her home, but he decided to stop off at the church and look at the graves. The name on them were, Colin Jane aged 35 and Marie Jane aged 3. Monique's name on each as wife & mother.

Now it was making sense because both had died on the same day. Was it possible that she had lost her family in the same way that he had? Had that event changed her life, like it had with him. He rode past her house then parked under some trees. Through the trees he had a clear view of her through his binoculars, she stood in the kitchen with her back to him. She stood in that position for a while then moved to reveal a picture on the wall of a man, with her and a little girl. It was a happy photograph with Monique's face glowing, very different to her stern face of today. Still very attractive, but in the picture, there was a warmth in her smile.

He went back to his camp with a clearer picture but more confused on what to do. He started to study the file again. Some of the information could be wrong or had been exaggerated, but the possibility of her ordering a shooting, just didn't add up. Killing the identical twin in error was a huge mistake, a repeat error would be his finish and a glamorous one would make headline news. He mulled over the day's events until he fell asleep.

Andy wanted to know more about her, so after routinely followed her to work he saw the receptionist, who had been about to leave her desk, with her purse in her hand.

"Morning! I'm sorry to be a pain, but I lost the note paper I wrote the details on. Remind me, is she a Miss or Mrs.?"

"Look, I'm supposed to pop out for a coffee for both of us!" she replied.

"Then let me get them as a thank you for helping me out, how do you both like your coffees?" she told him, and he left for the coffee shop just along the road. When he returned, he placed the coffees on her desk and she handed him a note, then she took a coffee to Monique. On her return Andy had looked at the note on which she had written Ms. Monique,

"Ms.?" he quizzed.

She whispered a reply, "Actually she is widowed, both husband, and baby were killed in a hit and run. Long before I ever started here, but I've been told that it hit her badly, and put her in hospital. A total breakdown by all accounts. She came out a different person, very different I'm told. Our cleaner has known her for many years and said that she went from angle to a demon after the accident."

"What happened?"

"After the hit and run was right outside their house, a man was arrested for drink driving, then banned from driving and fined but he had received no prison sentence. He was a son of a local politician, who could afford an expensive lawyer, who made sure he stayed out of prison. When she came out of hospital, she became a hard person, with a passionate hate for most men? But certainly, lawyers and politicians!"

Soon it was time to get back to work, so Andy left and went to the local library he wore a beany hat, pulled right down, hoping that he would not be recognise from the pictures on TV. Fortunately, it was exceptionally quiet, so he got on. He went through files of local news reports, until he found the hit & run incident of Monique's family. The date of the incident matched the date that she laid the flowers, the anniversary of their deaths. He found the report very detailed, it included the offender, and the name of his brief, a solicitor well known for getting celebrities off anything, including drink driving offences. He took notes, after which he quietly made his way out, making sure his face could not be seen by the CCTV. He went back to her office and sat on the grass opposite, he looked through the notes, until she went for her lunch, when he followed her once more.

Her routine was predictable, she was a neat person, everything she did was precise, he expected she was like this in business which made her proficient, maybe even feared. At the end of the working day he followed her back home, everything she did was like a carbon copy. He once more, spied through the windows using his binoculars, her movements mirrored her previous ones. With a gin and tonic, she stood and stared at the family picture on the wall for a while, raised her glass and toasted. Then blew a kiss at her husband and child, then retired to the living room where she drew the curtains to watch TV. He could just make out that she still had tears in her eyes, and a face full of remorse. He knew from experience that feelings such as those people could be bottled up deep inside, as she was, throughout the day and releasing inner most fears in private at night. But was it this that gave her a closed off personality, unable make friends, but organise others in a clinical fashion? To make and execute business plans, but unable to love. He could see that they had much in common, making her a target was becoming a problem, he wasn't sure anymore that she should be!

He needed the help of Marion Mayer, the reporter at the Gazette. She may be able to give him more information about her. His gut feeling told him to dig deeper and not to charge in.

Chapter 19

The next day he contacted Marion and she met him on an old band stand in the local park. It was deserted because of the heavy rain which beat on the roof, and danced on the paths surrounding the Victorian cast iron balustrade. The trees swayed in the wind as Marion shook her umbrella in the bandstand. With a bursting personality, full of confidence, she oozed coolness with a dash of spice,

"I wondered how long it would be, before I saw you again. You know you risk being caught meeting here like this Andy!"

"Yes, but I need your help. You can access information that I now can't. You know I was working to a list given to me by the PM and his secretary, both of whom are now dead. The last name on that list I fear maybe a mistake, she seems different to the others. Her name is Monique Jane," and handed her a note with her details on.

She stared at the wet note and battled with her conscience on whether to help, not only was her career at risk but maybe her life! But, her journalistic mind to uncover the truth, was winning.

"Unusual name! I will see what I can find out. I have several contacts and of course I will say it's to do with a totally unconnected story. How will I contact you?"

"Meet me here, same time, one week from today. Until then I will lie low."

Marion quickly left, splashing through the puddles, while Andy watched her, scanning the area to make sure no one was watching, or trying to follow her. He then followed her at a distance out of the park to her car. Once she was in it, she drove off and disappeared, he disappeared too, down an ally like a ghost.

***

For the next week he stuck to his word and stayed low, watching Monique from a distance. For him the time dragged by, while for everyone else, including the media. The week flew by, but he felt he knew Monique well now even though he had not even spoken to her. He knew her every daily move, habits and routines. He especially knew her face, every curve of her body and the way her body strutted with confidence and attitude. The only difference for everyone else, was that there were not any new murders by Mr. A., hitting the headlines. This was made up by, and kept alive with updates, interviews and repeats of the documentary, each time dissected by a different presenter with a different point of view. Each one stating that their view was the most accurate, trying to make out they knew Andy's mind.

Marion had found nothing unusual about Monique, except that when she approached people she had worked with in the past, they had no recollection of her. Considering her distinctive name Marion thought this was unusual. She had one other contact who worked within government circles of the secret kind. This contact owed her a big favour, and after a few days met her for coffee with her findings.

"I risked my neck getting this Marion. This Monique, it seems, may have worked for a while in intelligence, as a field operative 10 years ago. But as I say maybe! I found a person who matches her description including the family loss bit, but the name was different, she was possible given a new ID." She handed her the piece of paper with the notes.

Marion knew that this could mean trouble. On the day she met Andy, she relayed her fear, and he digested her warning, which made him more confused. It was possible that she was a plant, and still working for the security forces, but he felt that it was highly unlikely, considering her position within the company, and the fact it was 10 years ago. IF it was her in the first place. It all seemed very circumstantial at best. So, he resumed his observation of Monique daily. The more he saw her, the more he became convinced she was not a spook and shouldn't be the final target.

***

In the media, reports were starting to appear of copycat developments in more countries. The PM was under fire from all sides to catch Mr. A. and make an example of him. It was only a matter of time until these other countries would start to apply pressure, as their media pointed out that it was the UK where the new concept was born.

As each day went by, more reports came to light of copycats executing their politicians. Andy was not aware of this; he had been cut off from the media and the mayhem that was created. He now took on the appearance of a tramp once more, unable to wash, or change his clothes, worst of all he started to look as he did in the TV Documentary. He was out of food and money and had only a pistol to carry out his final hit, but still in two minds about Monique. So, he decided to do the unthinkable. It was 7pm and she had been at home an hour from work, he approached the front door and knocked on it. She answered wearing jogging bottoms and a baggy oversized sweatshirt,

"Yes!"

"I'm sorry to disturb you, but I've been living rough trying to find work. Can I do any jobs for money to buy food?", asked Andy

"My husband does all the work around here and he'll be home any minute."

Inside his head, Andy was kicking himself, for trying to pull off such an amateur stunt, he was a professional, what was he thinking,

"Of course, he does, I'm sorry to have disturbed your evening."

He was just about to leave when she said,

"Look, you'd best come in, the least I can do is give you a cup of tea."

Within 15 minutes they were sitting and chatting over a cup of tea, Andy felt a warmth building towards her soft voice and charms. She brought out some biscuits, followed by carrot cake, which Andy devoured. She then asked, "Hope you don't mind me asking, but you seem a capable and sound intelligent man. How did you find yourself like this?"

He answered with a lie and described a man from a novel he had read,

"I lost my job. Bills mounted, and I lost my home. With no address it's hard to move forward, no one wants to know you."

He looked around and saw the family picture adorning the wall,

"Nice family, little one not home?"

She then realised her little lie had failed, then tried to invent a cover story,

"Yes, they are my life. They are both out, but due back soon. My husband is picking him up from football club."

"Sorry, thought you said your husband would be home soon?"

"That's right!"

"It's getting late hope they're OK! You have family?"

"No. Both died some years ago." He could have bitten his lip, letting information like that out, it was a stupid mistake. Her eyes watered slightly,

"What happened?"

"I've taken up enough of your time and they will be home soon. I had best go now"

He got up and was heading for the door when she said,

"They're not coming back, I lost them some years ago. I'm sorry I lied. I didn't know you. I was a little frightened,"

"You still don't know me!"

"I'm a pretty good judge of character, and you don't seem a threat. Not as if you're this Mr. A. that keeps appearing in the press."

Andy was more than taken aback by that statement,

"I'm sorry, I know how it feels. Who's Mr. A. Sleeping rough, one tends to lose track on world affairs, and the news." he replied.

"He's a man that been killing off politicians, lawyers and rich people." She replied.

"Oh, right! Just as well I'm not rich then and I don't look like a politician!" he quipped.

"I'm home by six tomorrow, come back and I will have a meal for you."

He hoped she was going to offer him a bed for the night, as it had been a long time since he slept in a proper bed. That night was cold, and he started to feel really under the weather, or was it that he was feeling older! His army days being under canvas were long ago, his joints started to feel a little stiff. That night his mind buzzed with all the information on her, and her face burned into his memory. All was misted over by the warmth of her voice, and the mutual loss they had both shared, of family.

***

During, next day he repeated the same pattern as before by observing her now predictable routine, but he saw her through new eyes. While in the small park he noticed a bin with a daily paper just poking out of it. It was the day's paper, he retrieved it and sat to read it. Front page was a natural disaster in the States, page two NHS problems, and page three another politician had been found guilty of misconduct, just underneath was a woman displaying her womanly curves. The irony brought a smile to his face. Just below that, a similar article about a court case involving a lawyer. Page four was an article on Mr. A. It seemed to be a balanced view, much of which was taken from the short documentary made by Tom. He was pleased to see what he read, however, it also said that the authorities placed him at number one MOST WANTED. The working class liked him, but the upper class were split, the article said. It made him look in all directions. Was he being watched? Was the drunk sitting in a doorway opposite an agent, or the mother with a pushchair one? A man eating a sandwich a short distance away, was he an agent? Or, was he making a mountain from a mole hill? Time flew by because of his worries, but that following night he sat with Monique at the kitchen table, and enjoyed Lasagna. In her company his worries disappeared for a while, life seemed to have a normality to it. He felt like a normal average married man, not an assassin living on his wit's in a hole in the ground. He wondered if she would ever suspect him, then she said something that sent him cold,

"Were you ever in the army? It's just that my late husband was, and I see him in you, your mannerisms maybe!"

"No, I wasn't. What was he in?"

"Royal Signals. Communication and all that."

He wondered if he could have he been recruited by the security services, and leaving the services as a communications expert? Is this the link Marion had seen?

Then she opened a bottle of white wine, poured out two glasses and said,

"Your welcome to stay the night in the guest annex. It's only a converted detached garage at the side of the house, but it's comfortable, and warm. I've put shaving things and shower gel for you to freshen up."

He was now wondering if she was hitting on him, which made all thoughts of assassination completely disappear, and replaced with others, that he had not had for many years, awaking feelings inside that he thought had long died. He noticed that she kept filling his glass, but not her own. After four glasses he was starting to feel quite tired, so, she showed him the way to the annex,

"Beds already made and there's a shower where you can refresh yourself. Sleep well." As she went back inside, he watched from the window and guessed she was locking the door.

He took a shower and shaved, it felt marvellous. He was about to get into bed, when through the window he could see she was on the phone. He thought it was very late for casual phone calls, he went out and listened under the window, which was slightly open, and listened. He could just hear her,

"Yes, he's here, staying in my guest annex. I'm sure its him, he's dyed his hair, and is clean shaven, but those eyes match perfectly those of the video tape. I plied him with wine and food, so he'll be deeply asleep very soon. You're surprised I'm still doing this type of informing? I have expensive tastes (she laughed).

When and what time?

Roger that!"

He feared she was communicating with the authorities, so back in the annex he remained dressed, just in case. But surely, she's not one of them, he thought? Have I been wrong all this time or, am I misinterpreting, surely not? He felt gutted but hung onto hope that he had it all wrong. Two hours later he heard noises outside, he had previously made the bed look as though he was asleep in it, by using cushions off the settee. He had left his pistol in his dug out, so he took a lamp and ripped the electric cord out. Using the blade of the razer he made a slit in the cord and ripped out a single length of electrical flex to use as a garrote. A heavy glass ornament on the table was at hand if required. Now he waited at the door, hoping that what he had heard her say was something else, and not about him. He felt let down and hurt, the longer he thought of it, as he had let her into his heart. A heart that had been an empty void for so long. He could feel a presence outside the door, the hairs on the back of his neck stood up and a chill ran down his spine, which gave him flashbacks to a time of being stuck behind enemy lines. In a house with only darkness for company, outside those same feelings of an armed enemy about to come crashing through the door. But that was then when he was armed, now he only had his hands, wit's, a length of wire, and a funny looking glass fish.

The door handle started to slowly turn, and the door eased open. A pistol with a silencer came into moonlit doorway. The gun was followed by a hand, then an arm belonging to a man wearing a dark raincoat. Andy with breath held, waited to see if another would follow, as the man slowly crept through the bedroom door. There was another, but Andy sensed he was staying outside. The intruder was now in front, creeping towards the bedroom door. With the cord in a taught loop held in both hands, he quickly slipped it over the man's head and yanked tight. The gun fired. The gunman struggled and fired again as the man drew his last breath in a gargled gasp. Andy let him down slowly into an armchair. A professional would always use two bullets, and on hearing the distinctive two thuds his accomplice waited 10 seconds, then walked in and saw his companion slumped in the chair in the darkened room,

"Job done, good. No time to take breathers let's get rid of the body." He moved forward and kicked his foot.

"Come on you!"

Andy came up behind him from the shadows, as the man realised his partner was lifeless. But before he could react Andy brought the glass fish down on his head, the man fell into a heap. Andy then took the gun and shot both through the head.

He went to the house where Monique with her back to him, was pouring herself a drink, and two other glasses,

"You two finished then, poured you a stiff one each. After this I'm off abroad for a long rest." She turned to see Andy staring at her. His eyes, unlike before were now ice cold,

"Stiffs, don't need stiff drinks."

"Look! I'm sorry I had no choice." She replied.

"We all have choices! Thank you for your help in making mine up for me. I thought I could never love again." He said quietly.

"You felt that spark too." She replied, with her hand trembling making the scotch drip to the floor.

"Yes, there was a spark. For a moment, I thought I could live again. Maybe even love again. But you blew out that flame of hope." Raised the gun and fired. A hole opened between her eyes and blood spurted out. The scotch fell to the floor, and her body followed. Closing a hopeful episode in Andy's life. He felt colder now than when he first started his killing. He remembered the words he quoted in the documentary, was he going to hell? He thought not, because this definately was hell. He went to the music sound system and put on a track, 'What about Us' by Ministry, on a loop so it would be playing when the bodies were found. He felt it would set a macabre and cryptic setting for the detectives, which it did!

Chapter 20

The following day the media was buzzing with the news of the three deaths, due to a leak from the local police. Monique was known, but the two mystery men were not. A press release later described them as government officials, which started an assortment of stories springing up in local, national, and even world press. Conspiracy theorists were all putting fingers to keyboards and blogging their thoughts. 'Was this three hits in one go, by Mr. A?' one headline asked,

'Is this the end, or the beginning' said another,

'Which passenger is next on the gravy train?'

Each week saw a new copycat crime reported somewhere in the world, possibly others that were not. Murders involving political figures, or people in high profile positions became easy targets. Planned well, the evidence could point to Mr. A. or a copycat, before anyone else. Such was the confusion now; it was becoming hard to focus on the murder cases that had risen sharply in the past months. The press tried to make sense of it all by reporting sample cases, such as a wife who murdered her cheating lawyer husband, and leaving a note pinned to his chest saying,

"Regards Mr. A."

To which the police immediately suspected the wife, another story of the disgruntled sacked worker stabbed his wealthy boss in revenge, then spray painted a large letter A on his chest. It was said that maybe if they had researched the previous cases then they may have got away with it. But much of the original crime scene details had been kept out of the press, so no one could possibly copy them exactly. The papers described it as a virus that the UK was blamed for spreading to other countries, creating rebellious situations.

***

Andy had finished his list of hits, but Monique had rekindled his hate for the establishment, and authority. His stomach churned as though he had swallowed a bottle of vinegar, he felt sick. To him they rode rough shod over everyone born without a silver spoon in their mouths. The more he had found out about his targets, and the types of people they were, the more the hate grew. He was like a volcano ready to erupt and burn those guilty to hell.

***

The veteran soldier who was writing his story, from notes given to him by Andy, had finished and had no trouble finding a publisher, who saw this as pure gold. Marion was making sure things went smoothly, and helping with the publishing of the book. The publicity was huge and went worldwide, sales rocketed almost overnight, with orders taken over the internet, shops, TV, and newspaper advertising, even though the book wasn't yet out for another week or so. It was becoming the bestselling book of all time, translated into many languages. Marion had finished her copy for her story and was about to go public with, all she needed was a picture or two. But she had no way of contacting him, so, she made a deal with the author of the autobiography that if he shared a few pictures given to him by Andy, then she would plug his book in the article. Between them they would gain good money and make Andy famous, and maybe make people understand him better. But deep inside Marion saw another side to the whole story. Had Andy become just as bad as the people he was targeting. Indeed, it was true that his ideology was spreading, and world politicians, in various countries, were being murdered, if they had murky backgrounds to their characters. But there were even more reports coming in that some were just being killed whether good, or bad, using the ideology as a cover story. Mayhem was spreading. Andy's small idea had grown into a worldwide phenomenon that no one could control. It had morphed into an ugly cancer, with no rules or clear-cut purpose it had turned into anarchy. Riots were starting to form in major cities, if people felt cheated by the system, then they had the right to rebel, even kill. Andy had inadvertently created a standard in the shape of a monster, that every language recognized, and thought they understood.

'What's murder? When it's for a cause.'

Chapter 21

Marion's article was published the next morning, making her a star. She was asked to appear on TV shows, where presenters pumped her for more information to a degree that bordered on bullying, the very thing that Andy was against. Marion was uncomfortable seeing the side of human nature which Andy was seeing long ago. The internet fanned the flames of hate towards the corridors of power, no one was safe. Those in power, had suddenly realised they were the minority, as the masses grew. No longer were they afraid of the system, now the system was afraid of the masses, as they rose and demanded an end to political corruption, dictatorship, and the old world order. They were all in agreement, there was even talk of eliminating all religions which had been used as excuses to start wars, large and small. Pressure was brought to bear upon the Prime Minister to act and stop this epidemic of chaos. Placards outside Parliament demanding 'Charity starts at home' and 'End corporate corruption' and many others. The PM put an order out to find

Andy at all costs. Marion was to be brought in for question-ing, and a think tank was put together. They planned that by using the very media which spread the chaos, they would destroy and discredit all that Andy stood for. The secretary commented to the PM,

"This will not be easy!" one person pointed out!

"It's not impossible, it's been successful many times in the old days of the printed word, newspapers and magazines. The Americans are experts at it, so are we. Just get on with it. Fake news is our weapon. Use it!"

"What about Mr. A . . . Andy McIntosh?"

"Eliminate. Wiped him off the earth. I don't want anything to remain that includes the books, stop all sales immediately. He and his memory must be destroyed."

"I sense you hate him sir?" The PM spun round,

"Hate him, the man is a ruddy lunatic. However, his ideol-ogy was based on a sad fact."

"Sad fact? Sir" he enquired with an inquisitive raised eyebrow.

"The fact that there was corruption in our corridors, which he helped stamp out. There are dictatorships in the world, which the West had become decadent to. We ignored what our neighbours were up to. His way of dealing out justice was to execute the guilty, making himself guilty in the process. You and I, all of us in power know he is right, but we can't be seen to admit it. Just because a politician shags his secretary behind his wife's back, or, he snorts a substance to escape this rat hole of a world for an evening, does that make him bad at his job, no it doesn't? "My Mother used to say nothing is bad for you, if it's in moderation". After moderation comes greed. Andy was looking at those who abused that rule and got greedy. But now, the meek are getting greedy. It's our job to stabilize the world. Now get to it, and if you repeat any of this, I will have you shot, and deny every word."

"What word Sir, it fell on deaf ears. However, may I say Sir, that if that was made into a speech, it would deserve a standing ovation."

The PM nearly cracked a smile.,

In a police interview room, Marion sat opposite the chief inspector who put the newspaper article in front of her,

"I'm Chief Inspector Tom McDonald. This article is well written and includes so much detail, it's evident that you must have met him on several occasions. In fact, you admit to meeting him. So, my question is, where is he? How do you contact him?" he asked.

"I don't, he contacts me. I honestly don't know." The interview carried on for a further hour until the policeman left the room for a coffee. Inside, a female constable whispered to her,

"If you know, tell him. His chances with you are better than with the others."

"Others?"

The door opened before she could reply, but Marion felt sure she meant the secret service, who were past masters of making problems disappear, stories of many whom she had covered in the past. Seasoned very rich sailors had fallen overboard and drowned, editors who were powerless to convey anything different, other than the story provided by the spooks in suits. The policeman handed Marion a coffee and sat down,

"Come on Marion we know, you know how to contact him!"

"I did, I had a mobile number, which he has since disposed of. The last time we met he rang me, and we met in the local park…On the band stand."

He turned off the recorder and asked the uniformed officer to get two more coffees,

"Get two coffee's please Constable."

"But you have two fresh ones in front of you?"

He didn't answer, just motioned with his eyes for her to leave the room.

"I'll get two coffees Sir!" and she left the room.

"Look, in a fashion he did some good, and lord knows there was, and still is corruption, but he rattled the cage and made people listen. Now they want him, they will make a spectacle of him. With me he stands a chance, but the government boys will not be so considerate. They don't want him made into some sort of Martyr."

The door opened, and the police officer put two cups on the table, Marion had a sip, took a note pad out of her pocket and wrote 'Park tomorrow, 12noon. Come alone.' then handed it to him. He read the note, looked back with a nod and a wink. She knew he would be there, to receive an updated report from her.

The next day she stood on the bandstand, while Chief Inspector Tom McDonald entered the park. Up ahead he could just see Andy get up on the bandstand, and Marion greeting him,

"Andy please don't get mad, but a policeman is going to turn up in a moment, he wants to help. The secret service is after you, if not today, it will be tomorrow they will get you, and kill you. Please speak to him."

"You mean this guy that's coming?"

She turned, "Yes, that's him, Chief Inspector Tom McDonald."

"Good Scottish name!" he held out his hand to shake hands, and Tom reciprocated.

Tom went on to tell Andy that his option was to hand himself over to him. If not, the security services would take him, survival of which was nil. Andy was tired of the ducking and diving and agreed to go with him, much to the relief of Marion. She watched as Andy went with Tom, who was praying there were no government men watching. In the car Andy asked if they could drive to his house so he could get a change of clothes and maybe a shower. Tom agreed. In the house while Andy showered and changed Tom looked at his pictures on the wall and they chatted through the door,

"Nice family photos, I read what happened to them, I'm sorry. I'm guessing that it's that which started you on this vendetta."

"You guessed right! It's all in the book and Marion's article."

"You realise that all monies from book sales ... You won't receive any royalties."

"Yes, that wasn't the plan. The soldier who wrote it gets that. A victim of unjust war, by a corrupt government."

"Well the book is off the shelves, but the soldier did very handsomely out of that. What you started, got people thinking. Heads rolled! It even spread to other countries. People copying you!"

"Really! That wasn't my intention." he said solemnly.

"That's why they want you handed on a plate."

Andy shouted as the shower tried to drown out his voice,

"I'm not your average cold killer. I'm finished with that now. The old Prime Minister and I had a plan, that plan has been executed. Now it's up to them to get their house in order."

Tom's mind was in overdrive. Andy was a killer, but he believed that he would be no threat to society. He also felt that he wouldn't even see the inside of a prison. The suits wanted him dead. But he was powerless to prevent it, unless he was already dead, or, seen to be killed.

"Andy, I don't suppose amongst all your stuff here you have a bullet proof vest and a loaded gun?"

"I told you I am finished with all that, you're ok, I won't shoot you." He laughed.

"Not for me. For you!" replied Tom.

"You think when we leave here agents will be waiting to shoot me?" asked Andy.

"No. I will." replied Tom

"You best explain yourself, I came willingly, I trusted you!"

"You don't understand. From here I must take you to the city nick, not local. We must cross Carrington Bridge using the busy main road. Using your gun, we stage an escape attempt. We fight, I take your gun from you, I shoot you while you are wearing the vest under a jacket. You drop over the side into the river, if you can manage to stay under long enough and swim, witnesses will see you being shot and falling into the river, and hopefully think you've drowned."

"Are you a good shot?" asked Andy.

"Yes!"

"What's to stop you from shooting me in the head."
"Nothing! Except, a part of me wants to see you survive. I don't think you will carry on, but it's mainly because you shot a man that once raped my daughter at a party. An office party where she worked as a typist. She was 17 years old. He spiked her drink. But he used a condom, there was no evidence, only the vision in my daughter's memory of him laughing. Excuses were made, and she lost her job. His eyes welled up,

"I lost her a year later. Hanged herself in a wood near our home."

201

Andy saw his pain and remembered reading the story. Toms pain was very familiar to Andy, the type that does not go away. It slices through the stomach then heads north to the heart. A pain that becomes part of everyday living when something sparks related memories.

Andy went to a secret panel in sideboard and took out a black bin liner in the shape of shoe box, and put it into a backpack, then he retrieved another from under a loose floor board, and another from a false stereo speaker. Inside them was a total of £100,000 in cash denominations. While making his assassination hits, he had gradually pulled out all his cash from the bank, he knew eventually the authorities would seize his assets. With the money all wrapped in waterproof to protect it from damp, it was now going to get the ultimate test. Tom had not seen what he put in the bags as he had been in another room admiring photographs which adorned the wall of his military days and family. He then grabbed some clothes put them in a thick plastic bag and sucked the air out using a cordless vacuum cleaner then taped it up. That way it would not float well when he was in the water. Then Andy joined him wearing a false beard, and under his jacket he wore body armour. They rehearsed the plan. Andy armed with a revolver would be seen by witnesses on Carrington Bridge holding the gun on Tom, who in turn would snatch the gun off him, they both took several steps back, before Tom fired, and Andy would fall over the railings into the river.

They arrived at the bridge and Tom swerved the car and mounted the payment, as if a struggle had taken place in the car. Andy put an envelope in Toms pocket,

"What's this?"

"A five grand cash handshake. I'm not a bad man! Cheers Tom let's make this look good."

They burst out of the car, a spectacle seen by everyone passing in their cars. Andy pulls out the gun, and Tom leaped forward as per plan. Even the shooting was spot on, but Andy wasn't faking it much, as the two shots knocked him off his feet and over the rail into the river. Fortunately, the river was high, so the fall was short, the current was fast and pulled him away rapidly, meaning playing dead with his face in the water was more feasible. He floated down river heading south with the pack under his chest. Many things flew through his mind, to take him off the subject that he wasn't breathing. The water was thick and dirty, and he was getting desperate to breathe, he had gradually let all the air out. Then suddenly he stopped. He gradually rolled over keeping the bag under the water and played dead. He slowly opened his eyes. Andy was under the trees, in between bushes. He waited a few minutes to ensure no one was around.

Meanwhile on the bridge a few police cars had turned up. Within ten minutes others were on the way as Tom radioed that he had shot Andy, who was presumably dead. Shot twice at close range, he fell into a fast running river, with no sign of a body, he had surely drowned. Police started to scan the riverbanks both sides, while Andy was down river, and was now out. Andy hid behind the bushes and emptied the contents of the backpack. He changed into the dry clothes and put the money and wet clothes into a large carrier bag so as not to leave any evidence lying around. Then he ripped the zip and straps of the pack and used his pocketknife to draw blood from himself, onto the shoulder straps of the pack. He put it in the water, with the strap upwards and the pack was gently wedged into the bush, so it could be found. He started to quickly walk away along the bridle path, where he saw no one. Now clean shaven and clothed he didn't match the description given out.

It was twenty-five minutes until the pack with blood stains was found, which was convincing evidence that he was dead. Bodies could sometimes take hours to turn up miles downstream. Often, they would have been hit by boats, and props, making identification near impossible. Tom made his report, which was backed by ten witnesses, who all believed they saw Andy die. But there was a turn of events along where Andy left the river. A young policeman with a keen eye, and an interest in forensics, noticed just along from where the backpack was found, were a few tracks at the water's edge. He carefully edged his way towards them. He radioed for assistance, and described what he had found,

"Marks in the mud as though someone crawled out." He reported.

"That could be made by people fishing, a popular spot there." Came the reply.

"The rivers high, not ideal for fishing, murky water, and fast currents, plus there's no one here up or down stream, and these marks look fresh!" the young policeman replied.

He slowly followed what he thought looked like footprints, making sure not to disturb what he considered a scene of escape. He came to the bushes and could just make out that someone had been there very recently. It hadn't rained for several days, yet here, and under the shelter of trees, the ground was wet. There was also a single bare footprint. In his haste, Andy had missed these signs picked up by the young Sherlock. He reported his finding, and that he felt Andy may not be dead.

"I think he is heading south, down river." Then he was met by his sergeant,

"I hear you've found something." Enquired the sergeant.

He showed him just as Tom came running along,

"That could be anything, maybe some young lovers!" remarked Tom.

"But sir, there's the back-pack also!"

"Yes, I know about it. It's been bagged & tagged."

"Yes sir, but you shot him twice at close range. Surely there would be more blood on it, but it's no bigger than a thumb print,"

"You really are a sharp-eyed young constable; however, it's been in water, blood would wash away." He replied trying to convince all around him, as he was the detective. But the sergeant was not so convinced and radioed for armed back-up.

It wasn't long before armed back-up, and dog units arrived and were soon on Andy's trail. Tom was feeling sick to his stomach, he knew Andy still had the gun, and the units were extremely good with a high success rate. Meanwhile Andy found himself feeling melancholy whilst walking along the dirt path thinking of the time he and his wife would stroll hand in hand on a summer's day, discussing the future and home decor.

He thought he could hear a helicopter, looked up but no sign. Up ahead he saw a young couple coming towards him, it made him smile and wish he was young again. But he mustn't be seen, so he turned left, away from the river and started to cross a meadow. In the distance he heard a dog, reminded of a discussion he had with his wife, she wanted a puppy, so one day he took her to a rehoming center, and they got a german shepheard. Aged 3, rusty and bronze in colour, he made himself at home quickly on the couch, and on the bed, but it made them complete, until their daughter came along. That summer he made a white picket fence for the front of the house and planted roses. In his pocket was an old photograph of them he pulled it out and kissed it. This brought a beaming smile to his face, until in the distance he saw a policeman ahead with a dog, a sniffer dog. Then there was another. Andy turned and started walking back, but there was another, then another, coming from all sides. It was then the helicopter came into sight, it had been following him on thermal imaging. The police started to move closer and Andy looked at the picture again and said,

"I'm coming home love."

He pulled out the gun and held it under his chin then pulled the trigger, but nothing happened. A megaphone suddenly called out,

"Armed Police, drop the weapon now!"

But Andy looked at the picture, smiled and raised the gun. Two shots made birds scatter as Andy fell to the ground. With the picture still clutched in his hand, Tom ran up and fell to his knees,

"Andy, Andy." Tom checked his vital signs as Andy's eyes opened.

"I'm sorry pal, we'll get you to hospital, soon have you fixed up!" comforted Tom.

"I don't think so, in my house there is a letter to my solicitor, with instructions on my desk. I'm done now. My numbers up!"

"Andy, I suppose the A in Mr. A, stood for Andy?"

"No! A is for Architect, of a better future." His eyes became fixed in a stare, with a slight smile, as though he had seen something beautiful over Toms shoulder. Tom stood back up with a bag in hand and ordered a constable to secure the scene until forensics had bagged & tagged everything. It didn't take long until Tom was informed that the gun couldn't fire.

"I know." replied Tom.

"You know how? So, why hold the gun up as though to shoot, he knew it wouldn't work?" asked the policeman.

Tom smiled, "He simply just wanted to die. He would never kill a policeman or an innocent person. He only targeted scum. But now, he just wanted to be with his family again . . . now he is." and he was handed Andy's photograph of the perfect family.

"The irony is this meadow is known as St. Andrews meadow, after a church that once stood here, but was bombed during the war. Now it's Andy's resting place."

Then he noticed that there was no blood seeping through his clothes, so he took his jacket off and covered him, before anybody else noticed. A message was sent out stating that Mr. A received two shots to the chest.

***

At number 10 Downing Street, the Prime Minister was pouring out a large scotch for himself, and others who were all relieved it was over, but he surprised them all with a small, but strong speech.

"Gentlemen, a toast! I give you Mr. A. The biggest pain in the ass since Guy Fawkes. He was the enema this country needed. Yes, he assassinated colleagues, who were far less than perfect. But I will not let their deaths be in vain. Therefore, I will make it our duty not to slip back to the way things were before. Everyone will be held accountable and be totally transparent. However, we must not be seen to be condoning Mr. A. or his actions. This news I hope will help stem the copycat assassinations that have been happening. I also have it on good authority that it has worked in several of those countries as far as cleaning up a political system. But now the mayhem must finish, and a new political system will be born." And they all toasted a new beginning."

His secretary whispered to him, "Nice speech sir, let's just hope the seeds that have been sown by Mr. A. stay dormant, because if they should ever rise again, god help us."

***

Back at the river side they were still waiting on forensics, and the Doctor to arrive. The immediate area was taped off, and one young constable left with the body. The firearms policemen left the scene, along with Tom, who scaned the ground back to the river, for any remaining evidence. Tom made excuses to leave the body,

"He won't be going anywhere!" and had everyone backtracking for any remaining forensic evidence. About ten minutes later Tom turned to check that the constable was still at his post, he wasn't! He and the Sergeant went running back to find the young constable unconscious on the floor, and Andy's body missing. Tom opened Andy's bag he still had in his hand. It had wet clothes in it, but the bullet proof vest was not there, which Tom was expecting to find.

The Sargeant asked, "What's the matter sir?"

Tom smiled, "Nothing Sergeant, nothing at all, other than how can a dead man just disappear?"

A few weeks later in the Outer Hebrides, a cottage had been bought for cash by a big man with no family, who had sadly passed away and left the house to his closest friend. On the wall, above some photographs of his family and his past, was a framed letter from the old friend, leaving him the house, to live the dream that he could not. Living in solitude with an old 4 x 4 for transport in vast open grass land, where the sea breeze brought in the daily dose of salt air, that he loved.

He was living a self-sufficient existence. With solar panels on the roof, along with a satellite dish for communication, and media. A wind turbine powered a small workshop. An idyllic life for one man and his dog, a black german shepheard called Jimbo. His companions were the harmonious dreams of the night, and occasionally his friend, John Walker helping him through the night, well away, from the rat race, and rotten apples.

I hope you enjoyed this book, I always like to receive feedback from my readers, so please do leave a review on Amazon, it helps enormously! Thank you so much.

For more information regarding my books please visit:

https://roblambertbooks.co.uk

All books available on Amazon in both paperback and eBook formats.

Printed in Great Britain
by Amazon